A Not So Perfect Proposal

Holt Jacobs Mystery - Book 7

Lily Stirling

Cover Design by Mariah Sinclair

~ To both of my grandpas ~

While separate disasters befell your wedding bands, your marriages stood the test of time.

Contents

CHAPTER 1

Last thing I remember...I was on an airplane over the Pacific Ocean.

But now? I was lying face down with my head glued to a pillow.

I was no longer on the plane.

Was I in Australia?

It took a long time before I braved peeking an eye open.

Blankets were rumpled around me. When I raised my head off the pillow, a tiled room stretched out, with high windows. Maybe a basement?

Presumably this was my parents' home in Australia—the other option was I'd been kidnapped. But that was unlikely since I wasn't tied up and the windows weren't covered by bars.

I didn't want to move. Not only did I have a headache from a lack of caffeine, but my whole body was sluggish, and I felt horrendously dehydrated.

When I finally rolled over to the nightstand, my phone was there, charged and waiting. Since it's unlikely kidnappers are considerate enough to charge their captives' cellphones, it's safe to assume this was my parents' house.

When I tapped on the screen, I couldn't comprehend the time. My phone said 1:42 p.m.

Was that Australia time?

Since sunlight streamed in through the windows, it must be Australian time.

Melbourne, Australia, is almost twenty hours ahead of Seattle. Which basically means it is a few hours behind Seattle, except in the future.

How had I slept until nighttime for my Seattle body clock?

Before I could worry about that too much, the screen lit up with an incoming video call from my baby sister, Juniper.

"Hello?" My voice was husky. Over the video, my hair stuck out like I was a mad scientist, and my jawline was scruffy.

"Good, you're alive." My sister was way too energetic.

"Of course I'm alive," I grumbled, trying to smooth back my hair.

"Holt, what do you think of Australia?" Juniper asked, peering at her screen like she'd be able to spot a kangaroo.

"So far the only thing I can comment on is the bed I slept on. And"—I yawned—"I have no complaints."

"Do you know how long you were asleep?"

Why was Juniper rapid-firing questions?

"Dunno. I don't do math without coffee."

Juniper might have told me the number, but I wasn't paying attention.

Mom, in her infinite wisdom, decided that if I took a natural sleep aid partway through the sixteen-hour flight from LA to Melbourne, my body would trick itself into swapping time zones.

I was skeptical about the plan, my girlfriend, Brittany, was amused, and neither one of us wanted to deal with the comments Mom would make if I had a wacky sleep schedule *without* taking her advice.

With taking Mom's recommendation, I'd slept for maybe fifteen hours and woken up in the afternoon for my current time zone. Still, we'd tried out Mom's plan, and it wasn't my fault it hadn't worked.

But the bigger question was, how potent was the stuff Mom recommended? I have no memory of arriving in Melbourne. That's concerning, right?

I must've cleared customs, met my parents, and been driven here. But I have no recollection of anything past taking the sleep aid on the airplane.

"Brittany already showed me her room on the ground floor," Juniper was saying.

My suitcase rested on the floor beside me. I set the phone down and began unpacking the necessities.

"Her room's smaller, but since it's on the ground floor, there's a lower chance of deadly spiders."

Deadly spiders?

My hand froze as I held a clean shirt.

If I started scanning the room for spiders, Juniper would know she'd won. I needed to distract her.

"I'm surprised no one's barged in yet."

Juniper took the bait. "That's because Mom and Brittany are off adventuring. Dad stayed behind so you wouldn't be too scared when you woke up in a new country."

"Britt left?"

"And Mom," Juniper added, like she was afraid I'd missed that part.

"Why would Britt leave without me?" I asked, feeling strangely emotional...It was probably too much sleep mixed with not enough caffeine.

"Mom and Brittany tried to wake you up. The only time you showed any signs of life was when you called Mom a *monster*."

I nearly tipped off the bed.

How had the word *monster* slipped out?

Would Mom hold that against me since I clearly wasn't of sound mind?

I set the phone on top of my toiletries as I headed for the stairs. Juniper had begun monologuing about her social media career—it was like white noise in the background.

I'd planned on starting with coffee, but when I reached the top of the basement steps, there was a bathroom right by the landing. I decided brushing my teeth and a quick shower were the best way to kick-start the afternoon.

"Sorry, sis, I have to go," I said.

Juniper stopped talking mid-explanation of her dog Chouzie the Chow Chow's grooming habits. "All right. Love youuuuu."

"Love you too," I grumbled just loud enough for Juniper to hear before hanging up.

I'd say fate conspired to bring me to Australia. But I didn't need fate when I had my mother.

At Christmas, Mom began talking to Brittany about an Australian vacation. I was immediately nervous. There's not much maneuvering Mom can do in my life, but I'd walk barefoot over broken glass if Britt asked me to.

I didn't know how much damage Mom had done until Britt and I were planning a summer vacation.

My idea was a resort in the Colorado mountains. Britt could take me on a few hikes. Other than that, there'd be plenty of good food and opportunities to lounge around. Colorado was also where Britt lived before her dad passed away. I'd thought it would be nice for her to return to her home state.

Then Britt announced a plan to go to Australia.

You know how Australia is part of the Southern Hemisphere? That means their seasons are the opposite of what you'd get in the United

States. Instead of a mountain resort in the summer, she wanted to fly to Australia so we could experience their *winter*.

Britt wasn't worried about the weather. And Mom was happy to point out that Melbourne winters were mild enough that it wasn't a *real* winter.

I kept giving excuses to keep myself in North America.

I brought up what happened in college, the semester I'd studied abroad in Germany. The jet lag and massive time change nearly killed me. My first class, I fell asleep. And not like dozed off for a minute. I mean, they couldn't wake me and paramedics were called.

Mom had experienced my body's failure to switch gears when I flew back home. Yet no matter how much I reminded Mom or tried to convince Brittany that this trip was a bad idea, we'd ended up in Australia.

After my shower, I found the kitchen.

Dad was there, sitting at the breakfast nook, reading a book with pieces torn off from the cover and plenty of mangled pages. Where did he find his books?

Dad was so engrossed with reading that he didn't notice my entrance—and I was desperate enough for coffee that I didn't rush for a tackle hug.

It wasn't until I'd opened the third cupboard in my search for a mug that Dad noticed.

"Look who's alive."

"Hey, Dad." I cracked a grin. "Where are your mugs?"

In less than five seconds Dad had poured drip coffee into a clean mug and was hugging me tightly.

"It's good you're back on your feet," he said, like I was recovering from an illness and not a victim of one of Mom's schemes.

"Glad I survived." I sat at the breakfast table with my coffee.

Dad surprised me by getting me a glass of water and a plate of food. "You must be hungry."

I was starving. But what I really wanted was information on when Mom was bringing my girlfriend back.

If everything went according to plan, when I left Australia, Brittany wouldn't be my girlfriend—she'd be my fiancée.

The Australian proposal wasn't happening on our first day. I wanted to be clearheaded, instead of overwhelmed by jet lag. Still, if I could see her in Australia, that would make the upcoming proposal seem more real.

"When's Britt coming back?" I asked.

Dad had resumed reading. This wasn't rude or shocking, since our relationship was built on silence. Dad checked his watch. "Maybe an hour?"

Super.

I wasn't usually this antsy, but I needed to confirm Britt was on the same continent as me.

Dad and I fell into a comfortable silence. Him reading and me eating in between downing cups of coffee—and a few sips of water.

When I heard the slam of car doors, I assumed it was Britt and Mom finally back from sightseeing. But instead of the kitchen door opening, the front doorbell rang.

Dad frowned and closed his book. As he went to answer, I tried to read the book's title. The best I got was a partial image of a lion and the author's name, *C. S. Lewis*. Was he rereading the Chronicles of Narnia?

He'd read the series aloud when we were kids. I hadn't realized he enjoyed the books enough to read them to himself.

I'd just picked up the book to see if I could find the title in the interior pages when I overheard something more interesting than Dad's current read.

"...from the Melbourne police force. May we come in?"

Was Britt injured?

But that wasn't right. I'm not overly woo-woo, but if she was in trouble, I'd sense it.

My spot in the kitchen was hidden from the rest of the house. I picked up my coffee and tiptoed to the doorframe, trying to catch a glimpse of the officers.

Mom had hung a decorative mirror that gave a nice view of the living room. I watched as Dad led them inside and offered them seats. Unfortunately, the police officers chose the couch, so all I saw was the backs of their heads. Dad's reflection, though, was framed beautifully in the mirror.

I could hear them and watch Dad's reactions.

One of the officers held a small blue booklet out to my father. "Do you know this man?"

Dad opened the book, and his eyebrows shot up. "That's Holt. Why do you have my son's passport?"

My passport?

Automatically, I began patting down my pockets, like the passport might be transported from Dad's hand to my pants.

But I wouldn't have it on me. The passport should be in my messenger bag, tucked close to Britt's engagement ring.

Had I lost my passport? I tried to think back, but I had no memory after falling asleep on the LA to Melbourne flight.

The officer asked, "You're identifying Holt Jacobs as your son?"

"Yes," Dad said, meeting my gaze in the mirror. I shrugged, clueless about the officer's visit. "Look, what is this all about? Why do you have Holt's passport?"

"I...uhh...we..." the first officer said before trailing off completely.

The second officer spoke up. "We regret to inform you that your son, Holt Jacobs, is dead."

My mug slipped, shattering as it spilled coffee across the floor.

I was dead?

CHAPTER 2

Before I had a chance to react, Dad and the two officers crowded into the kitchen. One officer was my height, and the other was a good head shorter.

"Who are you?" the taller officer asked.

"I'm Holt Jacobs—the dead guy."

"Holt!" Dad raised his eyebrows at me like I was misbehaving. What did he expect? I'd laugh off my death notification?

"You're...Holt?" the shorter officer asked.

"In the flesh."

"This is your son?" the taller officer asked.

"Should be," Dad said.

The shorter officer held up the passport, comparing my face to the photo.

The picture was old. Back when I had shoulder-length hair and wore a necklace. Even though present-day thirty-one-year-old me was rumpled with damp hair, my current self was a total adult, while the person in the photo was a man-child.

"This hasn't happened before," the shorter officer said apologetically.

That was a relief. It would be bad if the Australian police regularly gave incorrect death notifications.

The shorter officer handed me the passport, and I flipped through the pages to verify it was mine. "Where did you get this?" I asked.

"This passport was in the pocket of a murder victim who bears many similarities to you."

"Okay..."

It made sense that if I was alive, the person with my passport was dead. Yet why was he murdered? And how did he have my passport?

"When did you lose this?" Dad asked.

I shrugged. That wasn't a question I could answer. Since I'd been allowed into Australia, presumably my passport was on my person when I went through immigration.

"Hold on," I said. "Let me check downstairs. My passport should be in my messenger bag."

Dad followed me down to the basement.

"Do you know what's happening?"

Dad shook his head. "No idea."

I'm aware my passport couldn't be upstairs with the police *and* be downstairs in the basement. Still, I had to check.

Had I lost it and the murdered man found it? Or had he taken it from me while I was in a sleepwalker's haze?

I went to my messenger bag and searched the main pockets. Inside were my laptop, power cords, and earbuds, along with random other necessities. But while I moved every item, my passport wasn't there. Next, I opened the outer pocket that usually only held a luggage identification card, and a small blue booklet slid out.

It said *passport* on the front.

Had my passport been duplicated?

But the emblem on the cover was wrong...There was a kangaroo, and it said *Australia*.

"Holt?" Dad moved beside me.

I shook my head. Even with a gallon of coffee, I doubted this would make sense.

I opened the Australian passport, and a stranger's face stared up. While I didn't know the man, there was a resemblance. We had similar complexions, and our noses were almost identical. But his sandy-blond hair was curlier than mine, and his eyes were blue instead of green.

"What's his name?" Dad moved closer to peer down at the text.

I didn't know the man. Why would his name matter?

But what I read made my neck tingle.

Last name, *Holt*. First name, *Jacob*.

Dad gasped.

We stood frozen, staring down at the words.

What did we expect? The letters to re-form into a name that wasn't a mirror image of mine?

A strange mixture of emotions came up. Yet the one I was most ashamed of was relief.

I don't know why my reverse twin was murdered—assuming this was the dead man's passport and there wasn't a third person in the mix—yet at least I was the one breathing.

Dad placed his hand gently on my shoulder. "We should go. The police are waiting."

When we got upstairs, the police weren't the only ones there.

Mom and Brittany had walked into the kitchen to find two police officers on their hands and knees on the floor.

The taller officer was picking up my mug's broken ceramics, and the shorter officer was wiping up the spilled coffee.

For a rare moment Mom was actually speechless.

The concern on Brittany's face disappeared when she saw me. All she said was "You're awake."

For a moment I forgot about the death and the stranger's passport. The only thing that mattered was Britt's return. I strode across the room and wrapped my arms around her before kissing her. "Missed you."

That comment roused Mom from her shock. "Missed her? What about me? I'm the person you don't see every day."

Britt shifted and pulled Mom into a group hug.

"Good to see you, Mom." I squeezed my arms tighter around them before disentangling myself.

"Why are there police on my kitchen floor?" Mom asked like they weren't in the room.

I expected the police to answer. They were silent.

I looked at Dad. He shrugged.

That left me with the truth. "The police came to notify next of kin about my death."

The shorter officer stiffened at my comment, while the other kept his head down, supposedly hyperfocused on finding every last shard of ceramic.

"Holt?" Britt asked.

"Is this a joke?" Mom asked.

"Afraid not," Dad said. "I left Holt in the kitchen to have the police tell me in the living room my son was dead."

Britt snorted a laugh. "You kiss pretty good for a ghost."

I winked.

Mom was less amused. "Since my son *isn't* a ghost, how did this happen?"

I stayed silent. The police should take the lead.

When neither of them spoke, Dad gave a pointed cough. Slowly, both officers stood up. The shorter man answered while holding the coffee-stained paper towels. "A man matching Holt's general description was found hit over the head with puncture marks on his neck."

That was new information. There might not be any significance to the puncture marks, but a blow to the head can be fatal.

"When cops searched the body," the taller officer said, "they identified him from this passport."

Mom took the booklet from him. She frowned. "That's Holt from a few years ago." Instead of asking the police further questions, Mom turned to me. "Why does a dead man have your passport?"

I shook my head. "No idea." Then, before anyone else decided to ask me questions, I got a new mug and poured fresh coffee.

Mom turned to Brittany. I knew that look. She was going full interrogation. "Holt was pretty out of it when we picked you up at the airport. Did you ever let him out of your sight?"

"No. Holt and I were always together." Britt's tiny scar by her right eyebrow grew more defined as she thought. "Or...he left to use the restroom."

"You're a paramedic. Couldn't you see he shouldn't go to the restroom by himself?"

I nearly choked on my coffee. "Mom!" This would be slightly less embarrassing if there weren't two police officers in the room. "What was Britt supposed to do? Hold my hand while I peed?"

Britt's cheeks were darkening, but she kept her cool. "We'd made it through immigration. Holt was walking and answering questions appropriately."

"But you weren't concerned about his altered mental status?"

Britt took a slow inhale. "It's Holt. We all knew this trip would cause disorientation, but he seemed capable of going to the restroom by himself."

For the record, this conversation about whether I was appropriately potty trained has to be the most humiliating thing Mom's done in the last seventeen months.

Mom was about to continue the argument, when Dad cut in. "To clarify, the only time you left Holt was when he used the restroom?"

Britt nodded.

"And this was after immigration?" I asked.

"Yes," Britt said. "You were in the restroom for long enough, I thought about checking on you."

Was that how it happened? Could Jacob have waited for an opportunity to take my passport?

In my sleepwalker state, I wouldn't have been hard to convince. Jacob could've entered the large airport restroom, held out his passport, and claim ours had gotten mixed up. Had I even checked the names, or had I simply handed it over?

But why would he want my passport?

"If you look at the airport footage," I said to the shorter police officer, "I'm sure you'll find I was in the bathroom with this man." I handed over Jacob Holt's passport with a flourish.

Perhaps it was unnecessarily dramatic, but these cops had given my dad a fake death notification. Nothing I did could beat that.

"Where did that come from?" Mom asked, crowding into the officer's space to get a better look.

"That's from my messenger bag. Our passports got swapped."

Mom pointed at the photo. "Was he behind you at the passport check? Maybe you were handed the wrong passport."

"Not possible," said the taller officer. "At immigration they only deal with one party at a time. The agent wouldn't handle extra passports."

"Holt?" Dad asked, not about to take the officer's word for it.

I didn't blame him. If Dad believed everything the police said, I'd be dead right now.

I shrugged. I couldn't remember the airport.

"Britt?"

Brittany moved to get a better look at the man in the passport. "No. I don't think so. In front of us was a ladies wrestling team, and behind us was an older couple."

The shorter officer brought the passport closer to his face. "This says he lives in Melbourne."

"Let's go check it out," the taller officer said.

The police were about to leave.

"Wait!" I called. "How will I find out what happened?"

The taller cop shrugged, and the shorter one said, "Read the papers."

Read the papers? Does anyone actually read newspapers anymore?

I followed the officers to the door, foolishly hoping they'd let something slip. When I returned to the kitchen, Dad was scribbling furiously into a notepad.

The room was silent, full of expectation. I refilled my coffee and waited for an explanation.

Dad grinned as he set down his pen. "I think I got it all."

I reached out, and Dad gave me the notepad. Written in his confident hand was *Name: Jacob Holt, Height: 6'0"*. The list continued with basic information.

"You memorized his passport?" I asked.

Dad shrugged. "I did my best. It should be accurate."

"Here." I pulled out my phone. "Let's see what Juniper can dig up about my Australian twin."

Mom shook her head. "He's a few years younger. That doesn't make him your twin."

I was saved from acknowledging Mom's comment, since Juniper answered my video call before the second ring. "A good arvo to you."

"Huh?" What was *arvo* supposed to mean? I looked at Britt, who shook her head.

"What are you talking about?" I asked my sister.

"The *arvo* thing?"

I nodded.

"I've been watching Australian videos to help you during the trip. *Arvo* is what Australians say instead of *afternoon*."

"Good to know," I muttered. Though a week-long vacation wasn't enough time to worry about picking up the local slang.

Calling Juniper was sort of a mistake because once I asked her to look up *Jacob Holt*, she needed to know why. Once she'd learned about the dead body and the passport swap, she had way more questions than I had answers.

Mom, Dad, and Britt added details whenever they could, but none of us knew much.

"Wait a second. Did the police return my passport?" I set the phone down, giving Juniper a view of the ceiling.

"I don't think so," Britt said slowly.

Juniper was abandoned on the kitchen table, while the rest of us began searching the kitchen and living room in hopes of finding a passport that said *United States* on the outside and *Holt Jacobs* on the inside.

"Call the police," Mom finally said, so matter-of-factly that you'd think a call to the police was part of our daily routine. While I've stumbled across a few dead bodies in my day, it's not like I have the police on speed dial.

I went back to my phone on the kitchen table. Juniper had remained on the video call. "Sorry, I have to go."

Juniper said, "Wait, I found—" right as I hung up.

Maybe I should call her back. It would put off asking the police about my passport. Then again, I didn't want to be stuck in Australia.

I called the cops.

Unfortunately, the officers hadn't left business cards. I spent close to forty minutes being transferred from department to department before I ended up on the voicemail for one of the men who'd notified Dad about my death.

I left a slightly rambling message, but at least I'd included my name and phone number. After I hung up, I realized I'd neglected to say I was calling about my passport.

I took a deep breath. So far, Australia had been plenty exciting, and I hadn't gone outside.

I sat back, staring blankly into space. My head was too fuzzy.

It really bugged me, but I had no memory of leaving the plane.

There were no time gaps for the flight from Seattle to LA. I clearly remember the weird sit-down restaurant we ate at during our layover. Then, as we waited to board, a passenger was having bad gas. I spent that whole time praying they wouldn't sit nearby on the sixteen-hour flight—that's a memory I'd be happy to have forgotten.

But try as I might, my last memory was sitting next to Britt somewhere over the Pacific Ocean before waking up in my Australian bedroom.

What had compelled me to trade passports? Had I done the swap voluntarily, or were they traded without my knowledge?

Why had Jacob been murdered shortly after the trade?

And, seriously, what were the chances that *Holt Jacobs* would cross paths with *Jacob Holt*?

I stared into a fresh cup of coffee. While I tried to make my brain work, the majority of my time was spent trying not to doze off into my mug.

Mom's purposeful stride into the kitchen had me blinking my eyes open.

"Are you ready for the restaurant?"

Restaurant?

"It's dinnertime," Dad said.

"There's no better way of showing you the culture than eating the local cuisine," Mom added.

I wasn't really hungry—especially for dinner—but I got in the car without complaining. It wasn't until I'd left the house that I wondered if I'd dressed appropriately. But I stopped worrying when I noticed my parents' clothes. Mom wore an exercise tank top, and Dad's shorts looked eerily like swim trunks.

While both of them were professors at the University of Melbourne, today they resembled retired tourists soaking up a new continent...If they suddenly clipped on fanny packs, I'd be leaving.

At least Dad seemed comfortable with the steering wheel being on the wrong side of the vehicle. He'd just reversed onto the road when Brittany's phone began vibrating in her purse.

"Hello?" she asked, then winced as Juniper yelled, "Where's Holt?" loud enough that everyone heard.

"Turn it on speaker," Mom directed.

Once Britt had clicked the button, I said, "I'm here."

"You're in serious trouble" was my sister's greeting. Before I could even ask what I'd done, Juniper added, "You told me to do a deep dive on Jacob Holt and then ignored all my texts and calls. Do you want the information or not?"

I rolled my eyes. "I've been busy."

In Juniper's background, there was a distant bark. "Hear that?" Juniper asked. "Chouzie knows you're lying."

Chouzie? Maybe it was the jet lag talking, but today her chow chow's name seemed extra stupid.

I didn't have the energy to argue with Juniper. Instead, I asked, "Did you discover something interesting?"

"Yes! I found out"—Juniper lowered her voice secretively—"that Jacob was a licensed snake wrangler."

Snake wrangler? That sounded like a made-up job for a character on a sitcom.

"And do you know how he died?" Juniper's voice was extra energetic.

"Murdered," I said. "Head trauma."

"Holt, the Melbourne police just issued a press release where they announced a man was killed after getting bitten by a rough-scaled-midnight snake."

"Murder by snake?" Dad called from his spot in the driver's seat. Dad was usually the *stuffy professor* type, yet when it came to real-life mysteries, he turned into a little kid. "Didn't the police say there were puncture marks on Jacob's neck? A snake bite would be a form of puncture."

"And the officers didn't actually say that Jacob's cause of death was a head injury," Mom added. "Juniper might be on the right track."

"But snakes?" I ran a hand through my hair, trying to hide my frustration. "This is Australia. Death by venomous snake must be common."

"In the middle of Melbourne?" Mom asked.

"Fatalities are rare," Dad said, then added, "The continent of Australia averages around three snake-related deaths per year."

Even Britt said, "The timing is suspicious."

"Yes," Juniper said. "The report said the venom was from a rough-scaled-midnight snake, a rare subspecies of rough-scaled snakes, which are indigenous to Australia."

"Did they find the snake?" I asked.

A dead snake wrangler was one thing. But a deadly snake slithering its underbelly across Melbourne was worse—and might negatively impact my day.

"Hold on..." Juniper mumbled as she presumably read more of the press release. "It doesn't say if the snake was caught. Only that they're gathering information from people who knew the victim."

"That can only mean one thing." I groaned. "The venomous snake is at large."

Juniper decided to be helpful. "Always check under the covers for snakes."

"Don't be silly," Mom said before Juniper got too carried away. "Your chances of running into a rough-scaled-midnight snake are very low. It's the spiders you should worry about."

"You're both hilarious. Goodbye." And I hung up the phone.

Britt's lips quirked as she tried not to smile.

"Mom's serious about the spiders," I said.

"I know." Brittany's eyes danced. "But she nailed the comedic timing."

I shook my head and grumbled something about wanting Britt on my side.

But being upset with Britt was mostly an act. Since I'd planned on proposing, there were plenty of times when I got so distracted imagining the future that I forgot how to be normal.

My mind was constantly going over the proposal plans. Aside from telling Mom to keep our schedule clear for the late afternoon two days from now and hinting to Britt about a surprise, no one knew the details.

I'd kept it all secret. I was proposing to Britt on the Melbourne Skydeck. The Skydeck offered a private engagement package that included photos. It'd be just the two of us, taking in the city around us. Sure, it's not the most original idea. But I don't know anyone in Seattle who's gotten engaged on the Melbourne Skydeck.

That view, that story, that moment captured on camera. It felt right.

Most importantly, I'd have my grandma's ruby engagement ring.

When my family first met Britt in Oregon, Dad mentioned giving me Grandma's ring if I wanted to propose to Brittany. At the time, I hadn't realized Dad was serious.

Truth be told, I would prefer to buy a new ring. A big fancy diamond that was an even bigger showpiece than Juniper's. Yet I knew Britt. She'd never feel comfortable wearing thousands of dollars on her ring finger. And she'd love joining the Jacobs family with one of our family heirlooms—assuming she said yes.

I'd asked Dad about the ring once I'd decided to ask Britt to marry me.

Dad had not only been serious about the offer, but he'd given the ring to my other sister, Casey, for safekeeping, since he had no way of knowing I'd end up flying to Australia to propose. It'd been an extra step, but Casey had mailed the ring to Seattle.

I had my girlfriend. I had the ring. I was in Australia.

All that was left was to wait two days, then go down on one knee on the Melbourne Skydeck.

My plan was perfect.

Chapter 3

The drive was taking longer than I expected. Dad had gone past multiple restaurants, but none of them fit into Mom's plan. This wasn't good. I've had too many questionable dining experiences while vacationing. What had she dreamed up this time?

My phone began ringing.

I frowned at the international number. Was it the police?

"This is Holt."

What followed was a string of sounds that I can only assume were words. Hopefully it's not offensive to say this Australian accent was too strong for me to understand.

"Uhh, hold on." I passed the phone to Mom.

"This is Gladys Jacobs." Mom was perfectly composed and didn't have any difficulty understanding the speaker. "All right...Let me write that down...Thank you very much. We'll see you tomorrow." Then she hung up and returned my phone. "That was the police station. We can pick up your passport tomorrow."

"Good." While it was icky to use a passport that was on a dead body, it was preferable to being trapped in Australia and living with my parents indefinitely.

"You don't need to look so relieved," Mom said. "You survived living with us for eighteen years."

I leaned back in my seat. "And there was never a dull moment, but now I'm pretty accustomed to my routine life." I glanced at Britt. "No offense."

She tucked an invisible strand of hair behind her ear. "I'm happy too."

If Juniper were still on the phone, she would have made a gagging sound at how over-the-top I was being. (Juniper is a firm believer that I'm *not* romantic and ignores anything that might mess up this theory.)

Since I was in a vehicle with my parents, the only thing that happened was Mom sat up a little straighter. Who knows. She might be planning baby showers for all the grandkids we'd have.

"Here we are," Dad said as he pulled into a parking lot. There was a restaurant with strong touristy vibes that was clearly what Mom had planned for dinner. The name *Crocodile Barby* was unbelievably tacky.

The restaurant was set in a small city square with decorative trees surrounding the area. On the other side of the square was a business that had the equally terrifying name of Reptile Pub.

"Why'd you pick this place?" I asked, a little annoyed Mom had chosen something so ridiculous.

"The University of Melbourne's campus is nearby, and I'm giving an evening lecture."

That made eating at Crocodile Barby a little more understandable. Still, I wouldn't have been caught dead in that place if Mom hadn't chosen the spot.

The interior lived up to my expectations of being extremely tacky. I once ate at a seahorse-themed diner with creepy critters staring up at me from all angles. But this place had the added fault of sound effects. Beyond the expected tourist-vomit decor, there were crocodile video games that kept beeping and zapping without anyone playing them.

Britt squeezed my hand. “How quaint.”

We were seated in a booth with a window that overlooked the square, giving us a perfect view of the Reptile Pub. The people going in and out of the pub appeared to be college students carrying books and laptop bags. Yet these students weren’t nineteen-year-olds with undecided majors. The people going through the doors had to be closer to my age.

“How’s Melbourne’s master’s program?” I asked the table, without bothering to check whether someone else was talking.

Mom’s eyes tightened, but she must’ve been glad enough to see me that she didn’t bother correcting my manners. “They have a thriving master’s program,” she answered.

“Are you thinking about getting a second master’s?” Dad’s eyes twinkled.

Before I could answer, Britt asked, “Second?”

Hold on. Britt didn’t know I had a master’s degree?

I was momentarily stunned. I was planning on proposing to Brittany and I hadn’t mentioned how many degrees I had? What else was I keeping from her?

“My middle name’s Ryan,” I blurted.

“I know.” Britt tilted her head, a spark of amusement in her eyes. “But about the master’s?”

“Uh, after my bachelor’s, I stayed and graduated with a master’s right after I turned twenty-two.”

Britt pursed her lips like she thought I’d said the wrong number. “Wasn’t that when you got your bachelor’s?”

I shook my head.

“Holt was twenty when he got his bachelor’s,” Dad said.

“Our college offered classes to high school students,” Mom added. “He got a lot of prerequisites done early.”

I rubbed the scruff along my jaw. "Sorry, Britt. I thought you knew."

She smiled, and her whole face lit up. "No problem. I'm honored to be with such an accomplished man that he forgets to mention how impressive he is."

I shook my head, both pleased and embarrassed.

"Why are the police here?" Mom asked, moving my focus from Britt to the window.

Sure enough, a police car had parked in the lot near Dad's car.

The car's overhead lights weren't flashing, and when the officers got out, they didn't appear to be in a hurry.

Dad leaned across Mom to get a closer look. "They're the same officers who came to the house."

While I hadn't originally noticed, Dad was right. They were the same cops. "Are they looking for us?" I asked, though no one at the table could know the answer.

But the cops didn't walk toward Crocodile Barby. They didn't even look in our direction. Instead, they disappeared inside the Reptile Pub. The name and old-world painted wooden sign had made me curious. Now that the police officers investigating Jacob's death were stopping by, the bar became a must-see.

"Fancy a nightcap?" I asked Britt.

Brittany didn't get a chance to answer because Mom jumped in. "We haven't even ordered. We're going to settle down and have a nice family dinner before I need to change my clothes and give my lecture."

I wanted to point out it was Mom who'd originally commented on the police car, yet I was wise enough to stay silent. I found Britt's hand under the table and prepared myself for a *nice family dinner.*

I absolutely hated the crocodile restaurant. While I did my best to fulfill the role of *loving son*, the constant sounds from the video games created a headache that only grew worse the longer we stayed.

Dad's eyes grew tight, and he began discreetly massaging his temples. Yet Brittany and Mom carried on a conversation like they were unaware of the atrocious racket going on around them.

I was nearing the *I may vomit* stage of sensory overload by the time Dad paid the bill and we were able to escape outside. The cop car was missing. It must've left during the meal, and I'd been too distracted to notice.

Mom's arms wrapped around me in a quick hug, and then she was off, moving confidently down the pedestrian walkway. I was about to lead the way to the Reptile Pub, when I caught Britt stifling a yawn.

She must be tired.

While I wanted to check out the pub, I also didn't want Britt to stay out too late.

I'm not sure how much sleep she'd had in the last twenty-four hours, but it was definitely less than me. I snuck my hand into my pants pocket to feel Grandma's ring box for courage.

It was impractical, yet I'd been carrying the engagement ring with me for the last nineteen days. Ever since the certified envelope had arrived from Casey.

But it's not like I was waiting for the *perfect moment* to spontaneously propose. With my luck, if I attempted spontaneity, I'd end up vomiting on Britt's shoes from a sudden bout of food poisoning. I'd puked twice on our first date. There was no need for a repeat performance when we got engaged.

Really, I liked having the ring with me, as a promise of the future I'd have with Britt.

But my pocket was empty.

A sharp pang of fear jolted through my system.

The ring was gone.

While I'd been aware it might be better to skip the pub, it wasn't until the ring came up missing that I jogged to the car.

What was the symbolism if the ring ended up vanishing?

My gut clenched—though that was probably due to the food at the Crocodile Barby. How could I be stupid enough to lose my grandma's wedding ring two days before proposing?

Dad and Britt followed. Neither of them actually commented, yet the underlying thought seemed to be *What's his rush?*

I tried to sit in the shotgun seat, yet when I opened the door, I was met with the steering wheel.

"You're not in Kansas anymore," Dad said as he moved past me and got into the driver's seat.

"Right." I gave a half laugh as I walked around the vehicle. Dad had no idea I'd temporarily misplaced a family heirloom.

Hold on. I was dumb. My brain wasn't functioning.

In the chaos of a thousand travel plans, I hadn't considered the problem of emptying my pockets to go through security. If I casually tossed the ruby ring into one of the bins, Britt might become suspicious. I'd put the ring in one of the zipped pockets of my messenger bag.

The ring was in my messenger bag.

My panic evaporated. I wanted to laugh.

I'd known where the ring was when I'd gone to check for the passport. How could I have forgotten now?

But...a new wave of dread twisted in my stomach. When I'd grabbed Jacob's Australian passport, I'd looked through the messenger bag. There'd been plenty of stuff I'd shoved in the bag, yet I couldn't remember Grandma's faded red jewelry box.

"Are you feeling all right?" Britt was leaning forward from the back seat, a frown creasing her eyebrows.

Just like I couldn't tell Dad I'd misplaced his mom's ring, I also couldn't tell my girlfriend about the missing engagement ring.

Beyond the obvious reasons for wanting the ring back, it raised an awkward question. *If the ring stayed missing, should I buy a new ring, postpone the proposal, or propose without the ring?*

I'd hate to propose without a ring. I know plenty of guys do that, yet there's something so slapdash about it. Britt needed to know I'd planned ahead.

"How much farther?" I asked Dad, anxious to check my bag.

"Around five minutes." Dad gave me a quick once-over. He probably thought I was experiencing traveler's stomach and was in desperate need of a bathroom.

While that wasn't a current problem, the food at Crocodile Barby had been greasy enough that future issues might occur. When Dad finally parked in the garage, it took all my self-control not to sprint for the basement.

Britt and Dad knew something was wrong, but I didn't need to act any more suspicious than I already was.

Once I made it to the basement, I immediately began checking all the pockets of my messenger bag. Nothing.

A cold sweat made my shirt stick to my chest. I might need another shower.

Hang on. *Shower.*

I'd showered and changed clothes today. Could I have put the ring box back in my pocket sometime after security? The ring must be in yesterday's pair of pants.

Immediately, I dug through the pockets.

More nothing.

No. No. No. This couldn't be happening.

What kind of idiot loses the engagement ring right before he proposes?

Since I'd checked the most likely options, I began a systematic search through all my luggage.

"Holt?" When Brittany found me, I was surrounded by empty bags and unfolded laundry. "Did you lose something?"

Her face showed concern, yet a lilt in her voice gave away that she was amused.

"I'm just, uh...looking for my nose hair trimmer."

My eyes must've gone as wide as Britt's.

Nose hair trimmer? Why had I said that? A nose hair trimmer is about as sexy as chewing with your mouth open. And whose nose hair grows fast enough that it's necessary to pack for a week-long vacation?

"Not, um...I didn't..." I tugged at my hair, trying to pull myself together.

Britt's laugh tinkled like tiny bells. "Relax. We're both jet-lagged."

"Thanks." I left my spot on the floor and wrapped my arms around her. "I just need to clarify, I'm not actually looking for a nose hair trimmer."

"I know," Britt said and went on tiptoes to kiss my cheek. "I can tell when you need a trim."

She giggled as she bolted from my arms.

"Hey!" I called, mildly indignant. "You don't get to run away."

Britt was still laughing as she jumped over my suitcase and ran around the bed.

I followed at a slower pace. "I will catch you."

Britt began backing toward the wall, her eyes dancing with the kind of excitement that only comes from being overtired.

I was within arm's reach, when suddenly Britt's smile vanished and she was crouching on the floor. "What's this?"

Yikes.

Had Britt found the ring?

I knelt down on one knee just in case I needed to make a spontaneous proposal.

But it wasn't a ring Britt picked up off the floor. It was a photo of two men printed on one of those fake Polaroid cameras. "Is this yours?"

I shook my head.

Where had it come from? I hadn't noticed the picture earlier. And it's not like I collect Polaroid pictures of strangers.

We crowded closer, both examining the image.

"Is that Jacob Holt?" Britt pointed at one of the faces.

"Uhh, sure." It more or less resembled the guy from the Australian passport. The lighting was bad, and the image was small. But since Brittany thought it was Jacob, she was probably right.

That might explain where the photo came from. It could've been tucked between the pages of his passport and slid out when I'd retrieved the booklet.

I bent closer to the picture. My focus wasn't on the men in it. Instead, I examined the background. Best guess, there were glass cages with heating lights behind alcohol bottles.

An icy sensation crept along my spine.

When we'd eaten at the Crocodile Barby, the restaurant was blessedly free of crocodiles, yet the bar across the street had an equally terrifying name...What was it?

Something to do with snakes?

"Reptile Pub," I breathed.

Could there be a bar with *live* snakes in Australia? Who would choose to go there?

But the police had stopped by, and Jacob was a snake wrangler...

Britt didn't answer—she was too busy yawning. I checked the time. It was around eight o'clock in Australia, which was the middle of the night in Seattle.

"Here." I took the photo. "We can talk about this tomorrow, after you get some rest."

Britt blinked sleepily. "I only came to say good night."

I wrapped my arms around her. I didn't want to let go. "Is your room nicer than mine?"

"A little." Britt snuggled into me. "But Juniper assured me the best part of sleeping on the ground floor is that it's less likely to have spiders."

"You're not funny," I growled, making Britt giggle.

We fell silent. I was sure Britt was about to pull away, when she asked, "Do you remember what we talked about on the plane?"

Britt sounded serious. She wasn't referencing the speech I'd given about the ideal size of airplane pretzels. I frowned, trying to figure out what she was referring to. Warmth spread across my chest as the memory resurfaced.

Right before I'd taken Mom's sleep aid, there'd been a child screaming on the flight. The kid wouldn't calm down, and Britt suggested I go to sleep. As I drifted off, Britt asked if I wanted children. Half-asleep, I'd said something ultra-suave like, "Sure, if you're their mom."

"I do." I rested my chin in her hair. "I remember what's important."

"Yeah?"

While no one's truly ready for parenthood, I'd take that plunge with Brittany. "I'll be ready."

I walked Britt upstairs and found Dad almost to the end of his torn-up book from the Chronicles of Narnia series.

"What do you need?" he asked, closing the book, sensing I was on a mission.

I showed him the photograph. "Britt found this in the basement."

Dad frowned at the image. "Isn't that Jacob?"

I nodded.

"How'd the photo get here?"

"Who knows." I shrugged. "Probably slipped out of the passport."

Dad nodded and began scanning the image, trying to find more clues. "Are those snakes?" he asked.

"I think so."

Dad let out a low whistle. "My guess is this was taken at the Reptile Pub."

"That's what I thought. Have you ever been?"

"No, but I've heard stories." Dad lowered his voice conspiratorially. "They used to have an eleven-foot boa constrictor, but it started strangling a patron and the owner had to cut the snake off before the person died."

Charming. Just one more reason to love Australia.

"Can I borrow your car and check out the pub?"

Dad's eyebrows shot up. "Are you sure? Isn't it getting late for you?"

"For once in my life I've gotten too much sleep."

Dad remained silent, analyzing me.

"Come on. I'm not even tired." Did I sound whiny?

Dad reached into his pocket and dug out the key. "Not a scratch," he said.

"Not a scratch," I repeated. Dad had been telling me that since I'd first gotten my learner's permit. If ghosts drive cars, he'll be telling my ghost the same thing two hundred years from now.

I almost went to the wrong side of the car but remembered just in time that the steering wheel was on the other side...It also meant I'd be driving on the wrong side of the road.

All I needed to do was successfully navigate a new city, with different rules of the road, and then I'd end up in the Reptile Pub, where I'd hopefully learn more about the murder victim who'd likely stolen my passport, while avoiding getting bitten by a venomous snake or strangled by a boa constrictor.

Easy, right?

CHAPTER 4

Overall, the driving went better than I expected.

Not only was I driving on the opposite side of the road, but it was also kilometers instead of miles.

You'd think it'd be complicated, but my brain is wired for engineering.

The biggest adjustment was leaving enough space for the left side of the vehicle. But that was nothing more than a real-world geometry problem.

I enjoyed the challenge, and it wasn't long before my brain switched over to the new driving rules.

Though it was winter in Melbourne, the temperature was a good fifteen degrees above freezing, which meant I didn't need to worry about ice.

My problem was, after I'd parked, I lost any motivation to go into a bar.

What had I been thinking? The Reptile Pub featured snakes and murder suspects.

I should be in bed. A night staring at the ceiling was preferable to trying something new.

I scrubbed my hand across my face. If I went back to Mom and Dad's, I could keep looking for the engagement ring. But I'd done a pretty thorough job tearing everything apart before Britt showed up.

How could I have lost my passport and my engagement ring? Those were the two most important possessions I'd traveled with.

Wait a second. I hadn't *lost* my passport. Jacob had taken it.

Could he have taken the engagement ring?

I sat up. That made the most sense. Even sleepwalking, I wouldn't have thrown a family heirloom into a garbage can.

Jacob must have taken the engagement ring when he'd swapped our passports. The police would have Grandma's ring with the rest of Jacob's possessions.

Tomorrow, we'd get my passport, and once I told them about the ring, they'd give me that, too.

I let out a slow exhale. It was okay. I'd figured it out.

My phone lit up with a text.

Juniper: *Dad said you're exploring the city by yourself.*

Holt: *Something like that.*

Holt: *Isn't it the middle of the night? Why are you awake?*

Instead of replying to my texts—which is the socially acceptable behavior—my phone flashed with an incoming video call from Juniper.

She skipped the introduction and asked immediately, "You really don't follow me on social media?"

"Right," I said—half distracted by a man in a baggy shirt exiting the Reptile Pub.

"Do you follow Chouzie?"

"What do you think?"

"Everyone loves Chouzie!" Her dog barked his agreement in the background. Juniper took a deep breath like that would center her. "Anyway, as I explained to my followers, this week I'm doing the Sleepless Nights Challenge to raise awareness for insomnia."

I couldn't stop my laugh. "Insomnia? The cause you picked is *insomnia*?"

"I'll have you know twenty-five percent of Americans suffer from insomnia."

"So?" I scrubbed a hand over my face. "How does *you* not sleeping help anyone?"

"I'm going to sleep a little." Juniper slowly inhaled—like *I* was being irrational. "But it'll show my followers how someone as vibrant and delightful as me can be negatively affected by a lack of sleep. It'll help people empathize with friends and coworkers who might be struggling."

"Good for you." Not that Juniper messing up her sleep schedule would benefit anyone. It's unlikely that my sister being cranky for a few days would positively impact society.

Face it, this was an online stunt. It wasn't like her motives were pure.

"Where are you?" Juniper asked.

"I'm in the car." I drummed my fingers on the steering wheel. "It's...I'm parked outside a bar called the Reptile Pub. There might be potential clues."

"Holt!" My sister gasped. "This is your first international case." Before I could answer, Juniper began clapping her hands. "Wait, a reptile pub must be the Australian version of a Japanese cat café!"

"Juniper," I groaned. "You're not helping."

"Do you want help? Ooh, I can be your electronic sidekick while you interrogate."

"What did you have in mind?"

"Put in one of your earbuds, and I'll be the wise-cracking voice in your ear."

"That's an awful idea" is what I said, but Juniper could see my smile.

I hated going into a snake bar by myself, but with Juniper on the phone, I wouldn't actually be alone. Plus, if she got too annoying, I could always hang up.

"Okay," I agreed. "But we're doing this on a trial basis."

"Sir, yes, sir," Juniper barked like I was a drill sergeant.

I winced. "If you yell again, I'll end the call immediately. Got it?"

Juniper gave a thumbs-up before I shut off my camera and got the Bluetooth set up.

It was a good thing Juniper called. Her online presence was the kick in the pants I needed.

The Reptile Pub was in a brick building without many windows. While I'd been expecting snakes, I wasn't prepared for *how many* snakes were inside.

Instead of a regular bar and tables, the whole back wall was cages of snakes with heat lamps.

"Mice," I muttered.

"What's that?" Juniper asked—I'd already forgotten she was in my ear.

I held a finger to my Bluetooth so everyone could see I was talking to someone. "Snakes eat mice. There's a lot of snakes here. How many mice do you think are in the storeroom?"

Juniper made a gagging sound. Ordinarily, I would have told her to stop, but I think she was legitimately sickened from my comment about a storeroom full of dead mice.

"Wouldn't that be against a food safety code?" Juniper asked.

"I have no idea what the rules are in Australia."

"I'm hoping *no dead mice* is a worldwide rule." Juniper's voice was extra high. Possibly her experiment with insomnia awareness was leaving her more emotional.

"Evening, mate," a burly man from behind the bar called.

I vaguely recognized him.

How was that possible? I didn't know anyone here.

It took way too much mental effort to realize he was the other man from Jacob's Polaroid. Who was this guy?

He must know something.

Since The Bartender was staring directly at me, I moved closer. "Evening."

"Another pint," a man called. "And a spotted python."

The bulky bartender had the beer ready and in the next instant was opening a cage and removing a garden-sized brown and black snake.

The customer took both the beer and the snake before returning to his table.

My jaw may have actually fallen to the floor.

Turns out, the Reptile Pub's customers weren't upstanding students getting master's or doctorates. They were strange humans with bizarre peculiarities that included mixing alcohol with carrying reptiles.

Very unsettling.

"What can I get you?" The Bartender asked.

"Not a snake," I blurted before I could stop myself.

The man nodded. His eyes crinkled with amusement. "Welcome to the Reptile Pub."

I tried to grin. "Never seen anything quite like it."

"Ask him about the mice!" Juniper practically shrieked into my ear.

I ignored her—I didn't want to know where the dead mice were stored.

The man nodded toward an empty barstool. "Have a seat."

I leaned gingerly against the bar. Snakes were everywhere. Most of them were in cages, though some were hanging out with customers. I wasn't going to accidentally touch one of those scaly creatures.

"Are you Holt Jacobs?"

I stared at The Bartender.

Had he said my name? Or was that a jet-lagged hallucination?

"Yeah. I'm Holt."

"How did he know that?" Juniper's whispering might be worse than her shrieking.

"Relax. I heard about you." The Bartender poured me a beer from the tap. "A friend gave your name. Mentioned you looked similar. I put two and two together. It's not like I'm psychic."

I actually sat on my stool and decided to tell the truth. "I didn't think you were psychic. I was worried you planned on killing me."

"No." The man slid his hand into one of the cages and didn't seem to notice the snake wrapping itself around his forearm. "Only the police think I'm a killer."

I blinked.

While I'd wanted to know why the police stopped by, I hadn't expected he'd casually bring it up.

"What did they want?" I said.

His hand in the cage tensed, but otherwise he remained calm. "Officially, they were making a death notification. Jacob was a student and worked here part time." The Bartender frowned. "But after, they took a photo of every snake in here and got copies of my snake handling permits."

I raised an eyebrow. Did he need a permit for each snake? How many permits would that be?

"Why do the police care about your snakes?" I asked.

Though we didn't have actual proof, Juniper was quick to murmur, "Because Jacob died from snake venom."

"You didn't hear?" The Bartender's jaw flexed. "Death by snake bite."

"I knew it!" Juniper's cheer echoed in my head. I wanted to yank out the earbud, but I didn't. She might prove useful.

"Snake *bite*. Snake *bar*." The Bartender's attention moved to the snake slithering around his hand. "After a lot of deductive reasoning, the cops thought I made a good suspect. Doesn't help that there was an incident here a few months ago."

"The boa constrictor strangling a customer?" I sounded too sarcastic. I should've kept my mouth shut.

His face tightened. "That story is over-exaggerated. Besides, it was a python, not a boa constrictor. Boa constrictors aren't native to Australia. It makes them illegal to own."

The snake slithered higher up The Bartender's arm, and I wanted to dry heave.

"You can relax," he said. "I'll tell you what I told the cops. None of my snakes are venomous."

"Sure," I said.

He wouldn't have venomous snakes in a place where customers were regularly handling them. Still, he must have a friend who could lend him a venomous snake if he asked.

"There's no other reason the police suspect your involvement?"

A muscle twitched in The Bartender's jaw. He took his time answering. "Look, I didn't know Jacob well. He's only worked here since May. But around a month ago he started acting strange. He got a new girlfriend. She was questionable. Ever since they started dating, something wasn't right."

Side note—yes, I realize it's judgy—what would a bartender with cages full of snakes and a freezer full of mice consider *questionable*?

The Bartender gently uncoiled the snake from around his arm before sliding the cage shut. "We argued about his girlfriend. There were a few times when customers were in the bar. Once, we almost came to blows. Cops were called."

In my ear, Juniper gave an excited gasp. "Find out the girlfriend's name. I'll track her down."

"What's her name?" I asked.

"Alexa Victors," he practically spat. "The name sounds fake, but supposedly she goes to uni."

"*Uni* means *university*," Juniper whispered—like she thought I couldn't connect the dots.

"I know," I said to Juniper, momentarily forgetting The Bartender was there.

He frowned. "You know about Alexa?"

"Sorry. I don't."

Juniper started giggling.

It was time we left.

As though sensing my decision, Juniper said, "Ask him about the passport."

I sighed. That suggestion wasn't half-bad. But I needed to get there in a roundabout way. "When I got here, how *exactly* did you recognize me?"

A customer ordered. The Bartender poured the beer before giving me his attention. "Jacob told me about a *Holt Jacobs* who was coming to Melbourne. Said this other guy was a slightly older, American version of him. What were the chances?"

What *were* the chances?

However unlikely, it was now beyond a reasonable doubt that my mirror twin had not only found me but had intentionally stolen my passport.

This raised a new question. How did Jacob know about me?

He'd stalked me at the airport. Had my passport gotten him killed?

It was a long shot, but I might as well ask. "Jacob took my passport. Any idea why?"

"No idea, mate. But"—he lowered his voice—"whatever the reason, I'm sure it had to do with his girlfriend."

It was approaching midnight when I returned to Mom and Dad's.

Dad had texted that Mom had gotten a ride home and the kitchen door was unlocked. I quietly let myself in, expecting everyone else to be in bed.

I nearly dropped the car keys at the sight of Mom calmly leaning against the counter, sipping from a mug. "Did I miss curfew?"

Mom set the mug down. "Don't be silly."

"How was your lecture?" I asked.

Mom asked, "Did you go to the Reptile Pub?"

Her question sounded like an accusation. But she'd taken me to a restaurant called the Crocodile Barby—she couldn't ride a high horse on my choice of a snake-themed bar.

"Yeah, I stopped by," I said, trying to slide past to get to the basement.

"Why would you go there? You've never liked snakes. There was a student who walked in, had a panic attack, and fainted."

"Well..." I actually didn't have an answer. Finally, I settled on, "I didn't faint."

Mom wasn't amused. "I've heard plenty of stories about that place. It's not a good spot to hang out."

A lifetime of experience had taught me it was best not to argue with Mom...but tonight I couldn't help myself. "Have you ever been inside?"

Mom's eyebrows shot up—she even placed a hand to her heart. "No way. Do you know what snakes eat? That place must have a freezer full of dead mice."

We'd shared the same realization about mice. Weird.

Was I starting to think like Mom?

"Stop smirking," Mom said, but I don't think she was actually bothered. "Are you heading to bed?"

I shook my head. For possibly the first time in my life, I'd slept so long that I wasn't tired enough to fall asleep at midnight.

Mom squeezed my arm as she moved to grab a second mug. "I'll make you some tea."

I sat at the breakfast nook. Usually, I dreaded one-on-one time with Mom, but that was because they were basically scheduled interrogations. This was unscheduled. Could tonight be a magical witching hour, where we could just hang out?

"Did you have a favorite...snake?" Mom asked, setting a mug in front of me.

"Nope. But I learned Jacob Holt was going to college—or uni—and worked at the Reptile Pub before dying from a snake bite."

"Oh." Mom's shoulders relaxed. "You went to that horrible place because you were investigating."

I chose to drink my tea instead of answering. Did she think I'd go there because of the ambience?

"And he's from Melbourne?" Mom asked.

"I'm not sure where he grew up, but he lives here now."

"Maybe he needed a US passport," Mom suggested.

"Could be," I agreed.

What had The Bartender said? Something about Jacob's recent girlfriend being a bad influence. Had Jacob gotten mixed up in something illegal and needed US identification?

"Without leaving the country, is there any reason you've needed your passport?" I asked.

Mom shook her head. "No. It hasn't come up. Once our work visas were figured out, we've only needed them for traveling."

Was Jacob trying to leave? If so, why couldn't he use his Australian passport?

"Do the police have any suspects?" Mom asked.

"The Bartender said the police were investigating him." I stared into my mug, worried my next comment would start a disagreement but decided to say it anyway. "He could be innocent. The guy seems...decent."

"High praise." Mom sounded amused.

I shrugged. It was a gut feeling, and I couldn't explain it any better than that.

"He'd be the obvious choice," Mom added. "A man who owns that many snakes is clearly comfortable around them."

I couldn't help shuddering with the reminder of all those scaly creatures in the Reptile Pub. "Such a creepy hobby." I fell silent, happy to sit in the peace of my parents' kitchen.

Mom, however, was ready to crack the case wide open. "If your bartender is innocent, do you think Jacob's death by snake bite was an attempt to frame him?"

"Could be." I sat back. "The two of them had public fights. He'd be an obvious person to set up."

In Australia, was this considered a bizarre crime? Or was snake venom a usual means for murder?

Mom's mug had the University of Melbourne's crest. Tomorrow I could look into the college angle. Who knows what might turn up.

"Will the university have an event about his passing?"

Mom's mug landed on the table with a thud. "You want to attend a candlelight vigil?"

I rubbed at the wrinkles in my forehead. "More, I was hoping there'd be an article about him in the student paper or a trending hashtag Juniper could follow."

Mom got up and brought our empty mugs to the sink. "I'll look into how the uni's handling his death."

"Sounds good," I said.

"Not too bad for a monster."

Mom let the comment sit.

What was it supposed to mean? Monster...Monster...*Monster?*

The blood drained from my face. "No." I pointed a finger at her—though I've been raised it's rude to point. "Anything I said while asleep cannot be used against me in a court of law."

"*Were* you asleep?" Mom raised an eyebrow. "You seem to remember calling me a monster."

"I don't remember." I scrubbed a hand over my face. "Juniper told me."

"Hmm." Mom sounded displeased, yet there was a sparkle in her eyes. Hopefully, she was just giving me a hard time.

I gave a cartoonishly big smile. "Love you."

Mom sighed. When it came to family, I rarely initiated saying *love you*...and usually when I did, it was to get out of trouble. Still, she couldn't help answering. "Love you too." She rested her hand on the back of my neck—a gesture that has calmed me down since childhood.

"It's late. We should get some sleep. Tomorrow we're off to the police station."

"Will do." Maybe it was the tea. Whatever the reason, I felt more relaxed.

At the police station, I'd get my passport and Grandma's ring.

With my passport, I could legally leave the country. With Grandma's ring, I'd be able to propose to Britt.

Things were looking up.

Chapter 5

I was being shaken.

When I cracked open an eye, Mom caught the movement. "Holt, you need to wake up."

I grunted—thoroughly unconvinced.

"Babe." Britt's hand mussed my hair. "You need to get to the police station. They have your passport."

Would staying in Australia be that bad? Absolutely no complaints about their mattresses.

But then I remembered, *The engagement ring.*

I sat up, grumbling incoherent words.

"He's alive." Mom sounded frustrated.

"Hurry and get dressed," Britt said. "They're waiting."

Once they trusted me to stay awake long enough to change clothes, I was left in peace. I checked my phone. 11:15 a.m.—late afternoon in Seattle. How had my internal clock gotten so messed up?

After I cleaned up, I met Britt and Mom in the kitchen. Britt held a giant thermos of coffee, while Mom had some sort of breakfast sandwich.

"You'll eat in the car," Mom directed.

I followed the two of them outside, a little amused they'd prepared my life's essentials.

My brain was pretty fuzzy as Mom drove. Not only does it take me time to fully wake up, but jet lag was clinging to me.

Today, the first stop on Mom's Australian itinerary would be a police precinct—she really showed off the best Melbourne had to offer.

It's odd, but while I've been a part of many murder investigations, I've hardly ever set foot in a police station.

Once we arrived, there was around forty-five minutes of red tape, further complicated by the fact I *didn't* have my passport...the very reason I was at the police station.

When we were finally escorted up an elevator and to the taller officer's desk, all he said was "Here" and tossed my passport on the desk.

His attention immediately shifted to his computer screen.

That was it?

I'd been forcibly dragged out of bed, driven to the police station, and done forty-five minutes of paperwork, all so someone could casually say, *Here*?

I took my passport but waited for the cop to look at me.

"Come on, Holt," Mom said, like she was worried I couldn't pick up on social cues.

I didn't move. Somehow I needed to ask about my grandma's engagement ring without Britt or Mom hearing.

I'd like to think that if I'd been more alert, I'd have known what to do. As it was, I was stuck between a cop who was ignoring me and my family wondering why I wasn't moving.

Finally I said, "Uh, can I talk to you for a second?"

Only then did the officer acknowledge my presence. He tore his attention from his computer, clearly expecting me to start speaking.

What was a subtle way of letting him know I needed privacy?

I gave a slight shake of my head—hopefully Mom didn't catch it.

The taller officer gave a half nod. He stood. "Coffee?"

"Yes!"

To be honest, I was more excited about a coffee refill than a legitimate excuse to leave Britt and Mom.

It didn't matter that it would be police station drip coffee. I desperately needed more caffeine.

"Back soon," the taller officer told Britt and Mom as he led me to a break room.

He filled a paper cup from the coffee machine and handed it over. It had the stale taste I'd expected. But I've drunk worse and was happy for the boost.

"We checked the airport footage. Your guess was correct. Jacob followed you into the toilet."

(I'm really hoping *toilet* is a synonym for *public restroom*.)

The taller cop stirred powdered creamer into his coffee. "All right, then."

It was my turn to speak, but it suddenly felt weird to ask a police officer if he'd recovered my grandma's engagement ring from a dead body.

"Did, uh, the deceased"—*Wait, I can remember his name*—"did Jacob Holt have a ring on him?"

The cop made a surprised grunt. "I'd have to check the evidence log. The only jewelry I remember is a stud in his left ear."

The coffee I'd swallowed threatened to come back up. I had to make absolutely sure. "I'm not talking about rings on his fingers. Was there an engagement ring with the passport?"

The cop's eyebrows shot up. "You lost your engagement ring?"

"Apparently so," I muttered, sinking into a break room chair.

"When's the last time you had it?"

My jaw ticked. Did he think I hadn't bothered retracing my steps?

I forced myself to sound calm. "The last place was in the LA airport." It'd been risky to check while sitting right next to Britt in the terminal, but I'd been stealthy about it.

"Have you called the airline?" the cop asked.

"No. I was hoping Jacob took the ring when he took the passport."

The cop shook his head. "If he stole the ring, he got rid of it before he died."

Or the killer took it off the body.

But the ring itself wouldn't be worth committing murder for. The value in Grandma's ring was primarily sentimental. It was a small ruby surrounded by tiny diamonds. Hardly worth the trouble of stealing and definitely not worth killing over.

"Was there anything else?" the cop asked loud enough to make me wonder how long I'd been lost in my thoughts.

"No, thank you." I shook his hand. "I appreciate your help."

"Good luck finding your ring."

I nodded. "Good luck finding your killer."

Britt and Mom were waiting by the elevators when I returned.

"How's the coffee?" Mom asked—clearly curious about my private conversation with the officer.

I shrugged. "The coffee was..."

"Disappointing," Britt finished for me.

"Yeah," I agreed. "I didn't get what I wanted."

It was early afternoon. Mom must've had a packed to-do list. Too bad for her, I'd need an excuse to hide out and call the airline.

The ring made it safely from Seattle to LA. But it could've been lost or stolen at any time after that. Still, calling the airline was awful. I'd choose being locked in a drunk tank before trying to reach the right person in an international airline's massive phone tree.

But my proposal was scheduled for tomorrow evening at the Melbourne Skydeck. I had a day to track down the ring.

We were still waiting for the elevator when the shorter officer led a woman around Mom's age and a college-aged guy to where we stood.

"Again, I'm very sorry for your loss. We'll do everything we can to figure out what happened to Jacob." Then the shorter officer left.

We all waited for the elevator.

I glanced at the new pair.

The woman was too skinny and wore heavy makeup. She was sick and trying to appear healthier.

The young man stood awkwardly beside her. They knew each other but weren't close.

Jacob? I mouthed to Britt.

She nodded.

The woman must be Jacob's mother, and the college-aged guy could be his friend.

Of course I wanted to find out details about Jacob. But cornering grieving loved ones at a police station was wrong—even Juniper would find the timing inappropriate.

I wanted them to speak, reference something that would be helpful for the case, but they rode the elevator down in silence and left in the opposite direction.

The three of us were quiet as we got into Mom's car. Through all the chaos of the past twenty-four hours, I hadn't considered that a mother had lost her son. That should make me less annoyed about spending the afternoon with Mom...right?

Instead of going home, our next stop was the Melbourne Museum. The exhibits were as interesting as every other museum I've been to—*that's code for very boring.*

I wasn't able to break free of Mom until late afternoon, when we finally got back to the house.

Once I was by myself, I called the airline we'd taken from LA to Melbourne. It took almost an hour of bouncing around multiple automations before I reached a real person.

"You're asking about a ring lost on flight QZA97?"

"Yes," I said to the actual human, right as there was a knock on the door.

"Holt, are you all right?" Brittany called—did I mention I was hiding in the bathroom?

Sadly, it was the only place that had guaranteed privacy. And I'd chosen to believe the phone call wouldn't last an hour.

"Hold on," I whispered to the airport associate, hoping she wouldn't hang up while I answered Britt.

"Uhh, yeah. I'm fine."

Britt asked, "Did you fall asleep?" right as I said, "Traveler's stomach."

There was an awkward pause. Britt and I stood on either side of the door, neither one of us wanting to break the silence. But I had customer service on the line, so I was the first to crack. "I'll be out soon."

It was a relief when Britt said, "Okay," and left her spot by the door.

"Sorry about that," I said. "Are you still there?"

"Yes."

Maybe it was paranoia, but from her tone, I got the impression she both knew I was in the bathroom and was judging me for it.

I mumbled something about needing privacy while the airline employee typed loudly on her computer.

"All right, Mr. Jacobs, the only recovered item on record was a smartwatch."

My stomach gave a sickening twist.

"Was there anything else?" she asked.

I managed to say, "No. Thanks for your time," before I hung up and dry heaved over the toilet.

Where was my engagement ring?

I could try calling the airports, but that would be another round of phone trees and long holds.

I dry heaved again.

How was I supposed to propose without a ring?

And how could I explain to Dad that I'd lost his mom's engagement ring?

Enough time had passed that Britt was standing at the door with her hand raised, about to knock, when I exited.

She frowned, defining the little scar by her right eyebrow. "Was it something you ate?"

Thanks to dry heaving twice and stress sweat, my *traveler's stomach* comment appeared true.

I shrugged. "Maybe."

"Do you want to eat dinner?"

"I'll try."

Mom had made her chili. It was usually one of my favorites, but tonight I served myself little and ate even less.

The police didn't have the ring. The airline didn't have the ring.

I could try the airports, but it was too late now for boring lost-and-found office staff to be working in Melbourne or LA.

Supper conversation went on around me, but I didn't pay attention.

Dad must've asked something like, "What happened today?"

Mom said, "Holt went to the police station, then spent an hour in the bathroom."

That caught my attention.

I raised my head, but Britt added for me, "We also went to the Melbourne Museum."

"And your passport?" Dad double-checked. "You can legally leave the country?"

I nodded.

Suddenly I remembered the taller cop's comment about *Jacob getting rid of the ring before he died.*

What if Jacob had proposed? Could his *questionable* girlfriend have the ring?

"Excuse me." I walked quickly to the hallway bathroom. (Since they already thought I had extreme intestinal distress, no need to come up with a new excuse.)

As I unlocked my phone, a warning flashed that my battery was running low—payback for my long call with customer service.

I needed enough juice to call Juniper.

When my sister answered, her face was unusually squinty. "Holt?" She yawned.

I couldn't help my laugh. "How's your insomnia awareness going?"

"Ugh, okay, you caught me mid–power nap. Not sleeping is no joke. It's like my whole brain's underwater. I was doing box-breathing exercises to relieve stress, and I must've gotten too relaxed."

"Drink coffee," I suggested and was rewarded with Juniper sticking her tongue out at me.

Real mature.

"Have you tried box breathing?" Juniper asked.

I shook my head. Around a month ago, that was Juniper's new shiny thing she'd been trying out. I don't know how many times she said, *It's really easy. Inhale for four, hold for four, exhale for four, and repeat.*

No idea what the big deal is.

A warning flashed that I had five percent battery left. My screen dimmed in an effort to conserve life.

"Listen, my phone's about to die. Did you do a deep dive into Jacob Holt's girlfriend?"

"Hmm...let me see." Juniper tapped a finger to her lips. "What did that bartender say her name was?"

I rolled my eyes. "You know I don't remember."

Juniper gave a melodramatic gasp. "My brother? Forgetting someone's name? Can't be."

"Whatever." I rolled my eyes. My battery was almost dead, and Juniper was wasting time. "Tell me what you found."

"Yes, sir." Juniper appeared to be mid-salute when my screen went black.

Figures.

Nothing about this case was easy. My phone dying was just one more thing on a list of problems.

I'd warned Juniper my phone was dying. I'd try her later and hope she was awake. For now I needed to rejoin the family and pretend I wasn't miserable.

I turned on the sink and splashed cold water on my face. My stomach gurgled, and for a moment I wondered if I'd actually be sick.

But I had to keep it together. Now wasn't the time.

I'd already retraced my steps and hadn't found the ring. It was time to retrace Jacob's.

He must've had a reason for taking an American passport. But how did he know I'd be at the airport? And had he stashed the ring before he died?

Maybe his passport was flagged and he needed a covert way of leaving the country.

But how was I the target?

We vaguely resembled each other, and it was odd our names were mirror images, but how did he know about me?

When I got to the kitchen, Dad was reading, while Britt and Mom were in the middle of a hushed argument. They fell silent at my arrival.

I set my phone on Dad's charging pad and waved at them. "Don't stop on my account."

Mom moved to stand right in front of me. "Are you too sick to walk along the Southbank Promenade?"

"It's winter," I said. "And you planned a walk?"

Mom's nostrils flared. "It's almost fifty degrees. No one's going to freeze."

"I thought a night at home would be wisest." Britt was slightly flushed.

I looked between the two of them. Then my stomach growled loud enough for everyone to hear. "Is my chili still on the table?" I asked.

"Yes," Mom answered. "You're not too sick to clear your dishes."

Britt's eyebrows shot up. But I wasn't surprised. I winked at Britt on my way to the dining room, trying to let her know I was okay.

I'm not sure why, but my appetite suddenly kicked into overdrive. Lucky for me, the chili pot hadn't been put away. I was ladling seconds in the time it took the others to join me.

Mom and Britt watched, seemingly stunned by my miraculous recovery, while Dad resumed reading a book from the Chronicles of Narnia.

I'd just served myself one final scoop of chili when I asked, "One of your kids visiting Australia must've been a big deal. Who did you tell?"

Dad looked up from his book long enough to say, "I didn't tell anyone."

That left Mom. Her nose scrunched up the same way Juniper's did. "I respect your need for privacy," she said carefully. "But my only son flying to Melbourne is newsworthy."

I raised my hands. "I'm not trying to fight. But I need to know who you told. Jacob was waiting for me at the airport. How did he know I'd be there?"

Mom nodded, conceding the point. "All the ladies in my book club know. Then, when I was volunteering—"

"Wait," I interrupted. "For now, just focus on people you told in...uni."

At that, Brittany gave my arm a squeeze. Was she impressed with my use of the local vocabulary?

Mom's eyes drifted to the ceiling as she considered my question. "Let's see. I generally don't share too many personal details at work. Uh...I told my teaching assistants."

Before I could ask for their names, Britt's phone began ringing. She answered on speaker. A moment later Juniper's voice echoed through the room. "Why isn't Holt picking up?"

All eyes turned to me. I shrugged. "My phone died."

Juniper let out an exasperated breath. "Well, I found Jacob's girlfriend. She's a college student and teaching assistant. Her name's Alexa Victors."

"Alexa Victors?" Mom repeated the name, then added, "Alexa is one of my teaching assistants."

That twist was big enough that Dad closed his book.

Chapter 6

Mom's teaching assistant was Jacob's questionable girlfriend?

I let out a low whistle. "That solves how Jacob knew about me."

"Does it help solve his murder?" Juniper asked.

I didn't answer. Obviously, it would be good to catch the killer...for justice and all that. But what I really cared about was figuring out what Jacob had done with Grandma's ring.

"When's the next time you'll see Alexa?" Brittany's voice was icy calm. Did she blame Alexa for blabbing to her boyfriend about my visit? It made me sit up straighter. Britt getting protective on my behalf had me feeling like the king of the world.

Mom checked her work schedule on her phone. "I'm supposed to meet with Alexa tomorrow at nine."

Did they need to meet that early?

Today I'd been forced awake after eleven. Could I be fully conscious by nine?

The best alternative would be to speak with Alexa tonight. That would have the added bonus of avoiding Mom's teachers meeting.

"Juniper, can you see where she hangs out?"

"Hold on." Juniper began humming as she resumed stalking Alexa's social media. "Okay, she has strong *naturalistic dark academia* vibes."

Did Juniper expect me to know what that meant?

Before my sister could explain, Mom jumped in. "Alexa's getting a degree in zoology with a focus on wildlife biology." Was Mom suggesting we walk into the wilderness in the hopes we'd bump into Alexa as she communed with nature?

Thankfully, Juniper's help was more actionable. "Recently, most of her photos were with her boyfriend at the Reptile Pub. But scrolling back, she spent a lot of time at one of the campus libraries."

"Thanks, sis," I said. "You're a creepy genius."

"I prefer *ultra-successful social media celebrity*," Juniper announced before I could end the call.

I sat back in my chair to find Britt's, Mom's, and Dad's eyes on me. "What?"

Mom broke the silence. "Did you forget the schedule?"

How could I?

"I know." I brushed back an unruly lock of hair. "I assumed the famous University of Melbourne library would be part of the schedule. Isn't that Dad's favorite thing in Australia?"

Mom's eyes narrowed. She hated switching up the schedule. But currently there was a semi-important location that her picky son actually wanted to go to.

Dad added, "There are a couple of books I need to return."

Mom opened her mouth, then closed it again. Finally she said, "I'm not actually a monster. But I did promise Brittany we'd stroll along the Southbank Promenade tonight."

My girlfriend stood. "Let's go to the library."

When Mom wasn't looking, Britt winked.

Suddenly I had the image of finding some abandoned corner in the library and making out with Britt deep in the stacks.

I needed to stay focused. This gooey-feelings thing had to stop. I had to find the dark academia girlfriend, get the ring, and give Britt a proper Australian proposal.

I asked Mom about Alexa on the drive to campus. The most important question was, did Mom suspect her teaching assistant was involved in shady dealings?

Mom's immediate answer was "No. The university does background checks."

Dad's cough almost sounded like a laugh, but he didn't comment.

"Did you ever meet her boyfriend?" Britt asked.

Mom shook her head. "No, I don't think so." She paused, her hands fluttering like she was trying to grab hold of a thought. "I saw him, though. The two of them were leaving the building together maybe a week ago."

"And?" I asked when Mom didn't give any further details.

She shot me a surprised look—I rarely asked Mom follow-up questions.

"It was strange. That guy kept looking around, and instead of a backpack, he was carrying a tote bag."

"This was leaving the building you work in?" I clarified.

"Yes. They were both leaving Gables Hall." Mom shook her head. "Who knew a dead body would make you so chatty."

"Maybe it's the brisk Australian air." I paused, considering Mom's information.

But Mom wasn't done talking. "Gables Hall has science labs on the third floor. There's admin and overflow offices on the second, and my department's on the first."

Britt and I looked at each other. *Science labs?*

Jacob had been acting suspiciously as he'd left the building, carrying a tote bag, and there were labs on the third floor?

If Juniper were here, she'd probably start bouncing with excitement and suggest Jacob had stolen a venomous snake from the lab, which later killed him...Actually, that wasn't a half-bad theory.

"Any chance Jacob stole a venomous snake from the third floor?"

Mom winced. "I'd rather not know if they're keeping venomous snakes in the building where I work."

"Would anyone be on the science floor at night?" Britt asked.

Dad said, "Doubtful," before Mom could reply.

Checking out the third floor in Gables Hall would go on tomorrow's to-do list.

As Dad drove onto campus, he asked, "Did Juniper say which library?"

"No...uh, the campus library," I said.

"The University of Melbourne has over ten libraries." Dad said the words with such love, it became clear his reason for switching continents had been the number of books here.

"I'm texting Juniper," Mom said.

My sister's reply was immediate. A moment later Mom announced, "Stephenson Library."

Dad gave a contented sigh. Apparently Stephenson Library was one of the good libraries—though it's unlikely Dad had ever found a *bad* library.

It's odd how driving through a college campus is basically the same wherever you go. The architecture was a strange mix of old and new, with a bunch of kids wandering around. And, yes, *technically* they were all adults, but eighteen keeps getting younger and younger.

Dad parked in an almost abandoned lot.

"We'll have to walk the rest of the way," Mom said, like we'd know how far that was.

Stephenson Library was maybe half a mile from the car. The building was brick and smaller than the surrounding structures, but it had architectural flair. The old building was updated to include card readers at the entrances.

"You realize Alexa probably won't be here tonight," Mom said as Dad flashed his campus ID and held the door for us.

I chose not to answer. Mom was right. In all likelihood, Alexa wouldn't be studying tonight. Still, I had to follow the few leads I had.

I was grasping at straws, but this woman was the best link I had to finding Grandma's ring.

"Study rooms are upstairs." Dad pointed toward the stairway, but he was already drifting nearer the shelves of books.

Mom's eyes sparkled as she watched Dad fall under the library's spell. "We'll keep an eye out for her down here."

I gave a thumbs-up as Britt and I headed for the stairs.

If we found Alexa, I needed a chance to speak to her without Britt. But I'd already lost Mom and Dad. I wasn't too worried about finding an excuse to ditch Britt for a few minutes.

"Do you know what Alexa looks like?" Britt asked once we'd made it to the landing and were peering into a study room with around ten students working inside.

What she looks like?

Okay, maybe my plan wasn't foolproof. At least there was an easy fix. "I'll ask Juniper to text a pic."

I sent Juniper a request for a photo. I received a video...and the video wasn't featuring Alexa. Instead, it was a thirty-second clip of Juniper listing the side effects of insomnia.

I replied with a string of question marks.

Only then did Juniper forward a photo of a college-aged woman with trendy short hair and the style of hoop nose rings that go in a bull's snout.

I zoomed in on her nose. "This should narrow it down."

"It does," Britt agreed. "She's not here."

There was another study room across from the first, but Alexa wasn't there, either.

One final door waited on the far side of the hallway. I took Britt's hand as we walked. "I love you."

I hadn't planned on saying that out loud, but from the way Britt's eyes fluttered up to mine and her immediate reply of "I love you, too," she didn't seem to mind.

I let go when we entered the room. The space was massive, with plenty of small bookshelves and little study nooks.

Here was my opportunity to separate.

With luck, I'd find and ask Jacob's girlfriend about the engagement ring without Britt.

"I'll search the left side."

Surprise flashed across Britt's face, but she nodded and moved to the opposite side of the room.

As I began looking, part of my focus was spent on making sure Britt stayed out of earshot.

I'd made it halfway through my search area with no sight of Alexa. True, if I didn't find her tonight, I could always crash Mom's work meeting tomorrow. But getting up would be a nightmare. Not to mention tagging along with my mommy is embarrassing.

I'd just cleared a small sitting area when a snuffling sound made me turn back.

No one was there.

I waited.

The snuffling happened again. I took a few steps closer and realized there was an alcove I'd missed.

Since whoever was back there was clearly crying, I was tempted not to check. But getting the engagement ring was worth the discomfort.

I walked quietly toward the alcove and peered inside.

At first all I saw was a woman's head bent over a laptop and papers, wiping tears from her cheeks.

The floor beneath me creaked, and her head snapped up.

I winced.

She had the bull's hoop nose ring between her nostrils and a face that matched Juniper's photo. This was Jacob's girlfriend, Alexa.

"Sorry," I mumbled. "Do you need a tissue?"

Why had I offered? It's not like I carried a handkerchief.

The woman squinted at me through bleary eyes. "Your Professor Jacobs's son."

I ran a hand through my hair, suddenly feeling self-conscious. "What gave me away?"

She blinked back some tears. "I, uh, saw your photo."

Mom was going around showing my photo to her teaching assistants?

Wait. No. That wasn't right.

Alexa was biting her lip and avoiding eye contact. She'd seen my photo, but Mom hadn't shown it.

"How did...?" I trailed off. Any minute, Britt would walk up. I needed to start with the most important question. "Never mind." I stepped into the alcove, disappearing from view of the rest of the library. "I know you were Jacob's girlfriend. I don't know what he told you, but your boyfriend swapped passports with me at the airport and..." For a second I hesitated. What if she didn't know about the ring? "And did he ever show you an engagement ring?"

"Engagement ring?" Alexa snuffled. "What did it look like?"

She asked tough questions.

"I don't know. Uh...there's a ruby in the center, surrounded by tiny diamonds on a gold band."

She wrinkled her nose. "Sounds traditional."

An argument could be made that rubies were uncommon in engagement rings, but I stayed silent. Partly because the rings on Alexa's fingers were highly *nontraditional*. One looked like the top half of a spoon had been twisted into a ring, while at least two other fingers had jagged-looking stones that Juniper would claim had *healing properties*.

Grandma's ring didn't fit her style.

My stomach twisted, and I took a seat on the bench next to her.

"Jacob didn't give you a ring."

"Yeah." She wiped a final tear off her face. "Are you sure he took it? He wasn't planning on settling down anytime soon."

"I mean..." I took a deep breath. "All I know for sure is that he switched passports."

A new emotion flashed through her eyes so fast I couldn't place it.

Before I could find a way to ask, Britt appeared. "There you are. What did—" Then Britt fully registered the woman I was sitting next to. "Oh, hello. I'm Brittany, Holt's girlfriend."

Alexa raised an eyebrow at the word *girlfriend*. I gave the slightest nod and hoped this stranger would keep my missing ring a secret.

"Do you need a tissue?" Britt asked, right as Alexa asked, "How long have you been dating?"

Britt was actually prepared on the tissue front. She quickly dug out a pack from her purse.

I answered Alexa. "We've been dating since last year's Fourth of July."

"That's an American holiday," Britt added.

I caught Britt's eye and tilted my head, hoping she caught the silent comment of, *She doesn't need to know the Fourth of July is a holiday to understand how long we've been together.*

"I'm sorry about your boyfriend." Britt pulled up a nearby chair. "Were you together long?"

Alexa's lips quivered, but she blinked away her tears. "I can't believe I'm crying. We just started dating."

"Death is always a shock." Britt's face softened, and grief filled her eyes. Alexa couldn't know, but Britt was showing emotions she usually locked away. Britt was letting Alexa see the woman who'd lost a father and a fiancé.

"Oh..." Alexa rubbed at her eyes. "Yes. Death is never easy."

I desperately wanted to hold Britt tightly and promise that from now on life would be perfect.

Ugh. What was happening?

I was supposed to be interrogating a suspect about a murder and a missing ring, but instead I was stuck making gooey eyes at Britt and wanting to let her know I was proud of her.

Even though I'm the happiest I've ever been in my life, this constant loss of focus was annoying.

Being in love is complicated.

CHAPTER 7

Britt and Alexa spoke for a long time about grief.

I'd mostly tuned out the conversation when Britt asked, "Do you know why Jacob needed an American passport?"

"Well…" Alexa's eyes went wide.

I leaned forward. "You must've said your professor had a son whose name was *Holt Jacobs.*"

"It may have come up," Alexa admitted. "But he never mentioned hunting you down in the airport. I have no idea *why* he died!"

Why he died? That was a strange emphasis.

Had Britt noticed? I glanced at her, but it seemed like she was waiting for me to ask another question.

"But you know *how* he died?"

I hadn't thought it was an upsetting question. By now it seemed like common knowledge that Jacob died from a snake bite. But Alexa's cheeks flushed, and she snapped her book shut, creating a cloud of old-book dust. "I have to go."

"Please wait," Brittany said.

But Alexa shook her head as she packed her computer and notes into her bag. She turned to me. "I'm sorry about your passport. But I had nothing to do with the snakes."

Then she was gone.

I let out a low whistle—inappropriate given we were in a library. "Why snakes?"

Britt raised an eyebrow. "At least it's not spiders."

"Really?"

Between the two, snakes are objectively worse than spiders. However, I didn't want to start a long debate. Instead, I wrapped my arm around Brittany, and we walked downstairs in hopes of finding my parents.

Dad was easy to spot. He was carrying a stack of books. The top one was open, and he read as he walked.

Behind us, Mom whisper-shouted, "What did you say to her?" The library door was swinging shut, and I caught a final glimpse of Alexa stomping away.

Britt answered for us. "We asked her questions about Jacob."

"That girl was crying." Mom huffed out a breath. "Honestly, Brittany, I thought you'd have a gentler touch."

I couldn't help my grin. "Yeah, Britt. You're supposed to be the nice one."

That comment pulled Mom's attention to me. "At least pretend to be bothered about making that poor girl cry."

"Hold on. Ordinarily I'd be devastated. But"—I raised my arms—"she was already crying when I found her. And she's hiding something. When we tried to get more information, she panicked and ran out."

Britt turned to Mom. "Did Alexa say anything to you?"

"Not really." Mom's nose wrinkled. "Maybe she muttered *snakes*."

I groaned.

Snakes.

If we needed more information about snakes, there was an obvious place to go. But I'd already been there once. Wasn't that enough?

Britt had other ideas. She rested her head against my arm. "Fancy a date at the Reptile Pub?"

"Sure," I said, while trying not to panic. "I thought you'd never ask."

There was a lot of discussion on whether or not Mom and Dad should join us at the Reptile Pub. In the end they decided to go home. Britt and I would hire a car to take us back.

I was about to enter the bar when Brittany stopped me. "Wait." She stood in front of me, her face serious.

I tried not to squirm. What was the matter?

"Be honest," Brittany said. "Would you be grossed out if I held a snake?"

My eyebrows shot up. "Do you *want* to hold a snake?"

Britt raised one shoulder comically high. "Only if it's cute."

"Then I'm safe. There's no such thing as a *cute* snake."

Britt's eyes twinkled. She let the conversation drop. A customer leaving the bar waited, holding the door for us to go inside.

There were fewer people in the bar tonight. It really highlighted all the brightly lit cages of snakes.

Britt took it all in. "I love it."

The Bartender's shoulders expanded when he noticed Britt's admiration. He offered Britt a drink on the house. Meanwhile, Britt's delight gave me momentary doubts about asking her to be my wife.

A question that should be asked in the early dating stages is, *Do you like snakes?*

Britt preferring tea over coffee was odd, but her enthusiasm for a snake den was concerning.

"Come on, sit down," Britt called from her spot at the bar.

I'd frozen at the entrance.

Obviously, I'm not a fan of snakes. But I also don't like *any* establishment that features live animals—it's why I avoid pet stores. If instead of snakes there were hordes of gerbils or dachshunds, I'd be similarly uncomfortable.

I'd just taken the stool beside Britt when a green striped snake slithered across the bar.

"Nope!" I yelled in a voice I didn't recognize and jumped away.

The Bartender pretended to be offended. He gave a brooding bad-boy pout as he leaned across the bar. "Your boyfriend's not a fan of snakes."

The stare Britt leveled at him could cause a heart attack.

He gave a nervous laugh and moved toward the draft beer. "What brings you back?" he asked, pouring me a glass. "Clearly not the ambience."

For a moment, I didn't answer. I'd locked eyes with a snake that was in one of the cages under the bar.

Once in Oregon, Mom had brought me to a nightmare-fueled seahorse-themed diner—it's actually where I met Britt—but this place with real animals was much worse.

"Holt?" Britt's eyebrows scrunched together, outlining her tiny scar.

I took a drink of beer, trying to collect myself. "How did Jacob feel about snakes?"

At that, The Bartender threw back his head and laughed deeply. "He worked here, didn't he? Had his snake handler's license. I'd say he liked snakes a whole lot more than you do."

I didn't reply. The only answers I could think of were rude.

At least Britt had more composure. "Did he apply to work here because of the snakes?"

The Bartender gave Britt his full attention. He drummed his fingers along the bar—getting dangerously close to her hand. "Jacob never mentioned why. The snakes were likely a selling point. Mostly, I figured he needed a job, and I was hiring."

"Did other people apply?" I asked—dangerously close to starting a staring match with a red-striped snake across from me.

The Bartender shook his head—decidedly less interested in talking with me than with Britt. "Plenty of people applied. I hired him because he had the most experience."

"Bartending?" I asked.

"Nope." The Bartender's attention was drifting back to Britt. "He had the most experience working with snakes."

What did my passport have to do with snakes?

And how did it relate to my missing engagement ring?

Britt leaned across the bar. "Did Jacob leave anything behind?"

My eyebrows shot up. Was Britt *flirting* with a witness to get more clues? (Hopefully it would work.)

"Nah, yeah," The Bartender said.

Did that mean *yes* or *no*?

At least The Bartender continued talking. "Jacob kept all his belongings in the top drawer of the file cabinet."

Britt's eyes fluttered. "Show me?"

He was only too glad to bring Britt behind the bar. I followed, playing the role of slightly jealous boyfriend. It was a perfect undercover role. He'd never guess I was an amateur sleuth.

The Bartender led the way through a door and into the back room. The place was a strange mix of office and storage closet. On one side, there was a desk and a couple of chairs next to a filing cabinet. The second wall was dedicated to toilet paper and cleaning supplies. The third wall shelved extra alcohol. And the final wall was set aside for all things snake related.

There, sitting beside a few empty snake terrariums, sat a large white deep freezer.

Dead. Mice.

A wave of nausea hit me. My stomach gurgled loud enough that Britt heard.

The Bartender was explaining how the drawers in the file cabinet could jam. Instead of interrupting, Britt raised her eyebrows to ask if I was okay.

I tilted my head toward the big chest freezer and mouthed the word *mice*.

Britt nodded. Seemingly unbothered by being in a confined space with a freezer full of mice remains.

"Here we are," The Bartender said as the top drawer slid open. "I have no idea what he kept in here."

A customer called from the bar, and he left us to look through the drawer by ourselves. He'd barely exited, when I whispered, "Since when do you flirt with murder suspects?"

"Mm." Britt tilted her head in an overly cutesy way. "It works for Juniper. Might as well try it out."

I stuck my tongue out—if she was going to act like Juniper, I could treat her like she was Juniper.

We began examining the items one by one and setting them on the desk.

At first the only obvious clue was that Jacob loved Nutella.

It wasn't until we got to the bottom of the drawer that we discovered a strange array of pamphlets. It was all stuff people shoved at students on college campuses.

When I spread them out, a pattern became clear. Most pamphlets had to do with international commerce and trade. But there was a smaller group devoted to animal conservation. The one titled "Remembering the Thylacine" implied a strange memorial service for an extinct species.

"Jacob had interesting hobbies," Britt remarked.

"Was he trying to start smuggling?" The words sounded far-fetched, yet what other reason could explain his actions?

I took photos of Jacob's personal items, taking extra care to get pics of each pamphlet. Finally, we put everything back in the drawer.

After the drawer clicked shut, I realized Grandma's ring could've been inside. But short of hiding the ring in the Nutella, Jacob hadn't left it at the pub.

As I exited the back room, there came a compressed sound of the chest freezer being opened.

Britt's eyes grew big. She let the freezer door fall with a thud. "You're right," she half whispered as she scurried to the exit. "There are *a lot* of dead mice inside."

I shook my head. "Why did you check?"

Britt shrugged. "I wondered if you were wrong."

"Snakes gotta eat," I grumbled.

When we returned to the customer side of the bar, The Bartender bent toward Britt. "Find what you need?"

"Maybe," Britt said.

The front door jingled open.

I didn't look, but Britt's eyes widened. "Alexa?"

That caught both mine and The Bartender's attention.

The Bartender crossed his bulky arms. "Jacob's not here anymore."

"I know." Alexa clutched a black bag protectively. "I'm here to get his things."

"Really?" The Bartender seemed to grow even larger. "Last I checked, a one-month relationship doesn't make you next of kin."

"But..." Yet Alexa was unable to finish that sentence.

"You're not getting his stuff," The Bartender said. "Now, I'd appreciate it if you left."

Alexa glanced around the bar before nodding. "Fine. I was trying to help. But whatever." She left without acknowledging me or Britt.

Why had Alexa stopped by? I'd seen the contents of Jacob's drawer. None of it seemed important...unless Alexa had a craving for Nutella.

The Bartender muttered something under his breath.

"Is she really that bad?" Britt asked.

"Depends," The Bartender replied. "She hated that Jacob worked here. She kept trying to get him to quit."

"Why did it bother her that Jacob worked here? You clearly care about the well-being of your snakes," Britt pointed out.

"Doesn't matter." The Bartender gave a humorless laugh. "She'll fight for any cause. That bull ring in her nose was part of some protest. She's opposed to the act of piercing animals to control them."

"She's protesting bull rings by getting one?" I asked—that kind of sounded like Juniper's *insomniac challenge*.

The Bartender shrugged. "Those hoops are a practice that's been around for thousands of years. Every civilization has found it humane. But it's one more hill Alexa's ready to die on."

Britt rested her hand on top of the bar, which was all the encouragement a small black snake needed to slither up her arm. She barely noticed, too busy trying to understand The Bartender and Alexa's varying perspectives.

I was bothered.

"Are we sure that's not venomous?" The words came out strangled as the snake explored Britt's forearm.

"Little high-strung, isn't he?" The Bartender directed his question to Britt. He reached over the bar and clapped my back. "Don't worry about your girl. I've got a business to run. Can't be letting venomous snakes into the bar."

I really didn't appreciate his tone—or that he'd touched me. Yet now wasn't the time to get defensive.

I wanted to make an intelligent comment about snakes, but I was drawing a blank. Hadn't I learned about them in school, or dozed through a reptile episode on the Discovery Channel? That information had to be stored in my brain. I just needed to access it.

Brittany was better at remembering fun facts. "How can you tell they're not dangerous? Don't certain nonvenomous snakes resemble venomous breeds?"

The Bartender's eyebrows knitted together. "That's right. But there are subtle differences between breeds, and I only buy from licensed sellers."

My attention ping-ponged around the different cages. There were so many snakes. How easy would it be to replace a *friendly* snake with a deadly look-alike?

Supposedly, all the snakes were purchased responsibly, but in the time Jacob worked here, who knew what trouble he may have caused.

"Why are some of the cages empty?" I asked, needing a distraction from the small snake that continued exploring Britt's hand.

"Aside from Mimi here"—The Bartender nodded toward the snake with Britt—"all the snakes are in their cages. They're probably hiding. Snakes like to burrow underground and hide for long periods of time."

I moved gingerly to what appeared to be an empty cage. Sure enough, there was a hole the snake must've made for more privacy.

"How do you know they're not missing?"

The Bartender's lip curled. He'd run out of patience with my strange questions. "I have a radar gun that I use to check the cages. Happy?"

Was that a joke? Weren't snakes cold-blooded? Did they give off heat signatures?

My voice was flat when I answered, "That's great news."

"We should be going," Britt announced, interrupting the stare-off I started with The Bartender. "Thanks for showing us around. This has been the most interesting part of our trip."

The guy winked at Britt. "Tell your friends."

My jaw tightened as I walked toward the door.

Had I really told Mom I thought The Bartender was decent? I took it all back. Who knew whether The Bartender killed Jacob—but it would be nice if he had. I'd love to wipe that smirk off his face.

Once we were outside, Brittany asked, "What was that all about?"

I wanted to ask her the same thing. She'd enjoyed The Bartender's attention a little too much.

"Holt?"

I needed to speak.

But I couldn't admit to being jealous.

I tugged at my hair and shrugged. "Jacob working at a snake bar wasn't an accident. With snakes liking to hide, could Jacob have swapped a harmless snake with a venomous one?"

Britt flexed the hand the snake had crawled on. "I hope you're wrong."

"But what if I'm right?"

CHAPTER 8

The house was quiet when we got back to my parents' place. Brittany did little more than kiss me and whisper, "Good night," before she went to bed.

Sadly, I was on a strange body clock and wasn't about to fall asleep.

Once I was in the basement, I checked and rechecked the photos of Jacob's possessions. Nothing jumped out. What had Alexa wanted?

Finally, I texted Juniper: *How's my little insomniac?*

She replied within seconds: *Terrible. I can't believe I agreed to do this for a week.*

"At least you're doing it for social media," I muttered.

Maybe Juniper sensed my sarcasm. At any rate, my phone lit up with an incoming call.

"How's Australia?"

That simple question made my shoulders slump.

"Did something happen?" Juniper seemed genuinely worried. "Are Mom and Dad all right?"

I waved a hand. "Yeah, they're fine." I sighed. As much as I hated to admit I'd lost the engagement ring, I needed to tell someone.

Who knows. Maybe Juniper would come up with a solution.

I confessed everything.

Juniper gasped at all the right places.

"It's bad." I wanted to pull my hair out. "The reservation at the Skydeck is tomorrow evening. I have to find the ring."

"And you called the airport?" she clarified.

"No, the airline. It took me like an hour to get the right person at the airline, and at that point Britt and Mom were worried about how long I'd been in the bathroom."

"Okay, you've called the airline, checked your bags, spoken with the police, looked through Jacob's belongings at the bar, and asked his girlfriend." Juniper's nose scrunched in concentration. "Let's see. I'll call the Melbourne and LA airports tomorrow, in case they have the ring." She paused again, lost in thought.

"But whether or not we find it, this time tomorrow you'll be engaged. That's a big deal," Juniper added that last sentence like I wasn't aware marriage was a life-changer.

"Yeah," I agreed.

Contrary to what Mom may have assumed, I'd never been opposed to marriage. I'd just never pictured meeting someone I'd want to share the rest of my life with.

Juniper clapped her hands together. "And you've thought it through? A full-time roommate. And not just any roommate, the kind that borrows your toothbrush."

"Ugh!" I half choked on air. "We'll *never* share a toothbrush."

"What if—"

"Never."

I might be ready to share my life with Brittany. However, I'd stop brushing my teeth before I *ever* share a toothbrush with *anyone*.

Juniper peered into the camera. "You're turning green. Relax, it's just a toothbrush."

If my sister didn't instinctively know how disgusting her suggestion was, there was no use explaining it.

"About my missing ring?"

"Right, sorry." Juniper rubbed at her eyes. "Lack of sleep is making me scatterbrained. You're sure Jacob's girlfriend was telling the truth about the ring?"

"Yeah." My answer was immediate. "She said their relationship wasn't serious. And"—I lowered my voice—"Grandma's ring wasn't her style."

Juniper giggled. "And you're sure the ring is Brittany's style?"

My sister's real question was *Why don't you buy her a giant rock?*

I raised an eyebrow. "Britt prefers heartfelt over showy."

"Sure she does."

I let the subject drop. When it came to engagement rings, I wouldn't be able to convince my sister that *bigger* didn't always mean *better.*

Juniper loved the massive stone that weighed down her ring finger. Every compliment made her feel that much better about her status. Yet Britt would hate strangers commenting on her jewelry.

"It's strange, though," I said, hoping to distract Juniper. "The Bartender mentioned Jacob's girlfriend was a *bad influence*, but she seemed pretty normal. Just another college kid ready to change the world."

"Because you're such a good judge of character?"

I frowned at the phone. "She's Mom's teaching assistant."

"Right." Juniper's shoulders slumped in disappointment. "It would be difficult to hide any deep dark secrets from Mom."

"Exactly," I agreed. "The question becomes, was The Bartender trying to throw suspicion off himself, or was he wrong about the girlfriend?"

"My dear Watson"—Juniper attempted a cringey British accent—"that's indubitably a brilliant question."

"Thank you." I tried to accept the compliment without getting annoyed by Juniper's over-the-top behavior. "Look, Jacob worked at the Reptile Pub since May. His boss noticed a difference in his behavior around the time he started dating his girlfriend."

Juniper was researching on her end. "Looks like the first photo of Jacob and Alexa together is from July."

Juniper's eyebrows creased, and she bent closer to the screen. "That's strange. He started posting photos around Gables Hall at least a month before his relationship with Alexa."

"Huh." What could that mean? "It's possible Jacob met his girlfriend while doing some shady activity."

"Precisely." Juniper clapped her hands together, seeming a little *too* proud of herself.

I sat back against the bed. "Mom mentioned the third floor of the building is for science. Can you find out what specifically they do?"

That actually took Juniper some time to discover. I began resting my eyes as my sister mumbled about *archaic university websites.*

"Holt!" Juniper's yell woke me up.

"Sorry," I muttered.

I expected Juniper to go on a self-righteous rant about how she was sacrificing her own sleep to raise awareness.

She chose a different route. "Look, if sleep is more important than catching a killer, maybe we should call it a night."

I didn't answer. Juniper knew me well enough to resume talking—after she'd waited an appropriate amount of time to let me *deeply consider her words.*

"Broadly, the third floor of Gables Hall is for biology. Then let's see...This semester there's a visiting professor from the United States who specializes in"—Juniper paused, trying to create suspense—"reptiles."

I rubbed at my forehead. Jet-lag fuzziness was creeping in. "Aren't the Melbourne semesters different from schools in the US?"

Juniper shrugged. "Probably." She tapped on her phone. "Yes. This semester started in July, almost four weeks ago."

"And that's when Jacob started dating his new girlfriend?"

"Yup," Juniper agreed.

"Alexa might not have anything to do with it," I said. "Jacob's behavior could've changed because of the new semester."

"It's the professor!" Juniper squealed.

I sighed. Must she be this loud?

"Possibly," I said. "Looking at the timeline, a new professor from the United States shows up specializing in reptiles. Around that time Jacob starts behaving strangely. Fast-forward a few weeks and he's found dead with a stolen passport."

Juniper's eyes had glazed over. "I'm way too tired for this."

I got up and began pacing. This new information was strangely energizing. "I'll need to go to work with Mom."

"Mmm," Juniper agreed, her eyes mostly shut.

"Is there a photo of The Professor?"

Juniper's answer was a noise that sounded suspiciously like a snore. I must've been hearing things because, according to my sister, she doesn't snore.

I hung up, then proceeded to spend the next hour trying to find the name of the visiting professor.

Had Juniper given the name?

I couldn't remember.

My energy was beginning to fade when I finally found Professor Rhys. His face was almost reptilian, with squinty eyes like he'd spent too much time staring at the sun.

This is pure speculation based on physical features, but between The Bartender, Alexa, and Professor Rhys, The Professor was the most suspicious of the bunch.

It was well past two a.m. Melbourne time when I turned in.

I'd be a bear to wake up, but I left a note on the coffee maker requesting to go to campus with Mom.

I needed to meet Professor Rhys and figure out what role he'd played in Jacob's life—and whether he was involved in Jacob's death.

Juniper would contact the airports about the engagement ring. Tomorrow morning my priority could be solving a murder.

Giving Juniper a chance to do her thing with Britt's ring seemed reasonable. Yet as I lay in bed, instead of my brain focusing on the mystery, all I could concentrate on was how badly I wanted Britt as my wife.

Here's the thing.

My first memory of the morning was waking up sprawled across the back seat of Mom's car with a thermos of coffee clutched to my heart like I was a toddler holding a teddy bear.

Teddy bear? Britt asks about kids once, and all of a sudden I'm thinking like a dad.

The vehicle wasn't moving, and the sky was bright.

"Mom?" I croaked—not that I actually expected her to sit around waiting when she had a job to do.

"Morning." The voice was Britt's.

I grinned and sat up.

Britt sat in the front passenger seat holding one of Dad's books from the Chronicles of Narnia.

"You saw my note?" I leaned across the seat for an awkward kiss.

Britt's lips trembled against mine as she laughed. "Do you have any idea what it was like getting you to the car?"

I shrugged. Seeing as I had no recollection, my guess was I'd been unresponsive.

My back was cramped from lying on the seats. I half stumbled out of the car before leaning against the hood and gulping down coffee.

Britt bumped my shoulder as she settled beside me.

Who knows how, but I was actually wearing clothes. I had on a pair of slacks, a shirt, and even a light jacket. Mom was right—the Australian winter was well above freezing. I may have been dressed, but my breath couldn't be described as *minty*.

"I take it I didn't brush my teeth?"

Britt nodded.

"And my hair?"

"A poofy mess."

I winced. "Figures."

"Hold on." Britt reopened the car door and reappeared with one of those nondescript tourist hats...not a cowboy hat, could be a misshapen bucket hat, yet somehow belonged on a safari. "I grabbed this on the way out."

"It's Dad's?" I couldn't help the question. Back in the States, he'd never owned anything that tacky.

Out of curiosity, I put the hat on.

"How do I look?" I gave my best brooding model pout.

"Very sexy." She giggled. "You'll be the next big heartthrob."

"I'll bet."

I tossed the hat back in the car. I couldn't be in public with that monstrosity on my head. But I didn't want my humidified hair sticking out in strange directions. "Is there any water?"

Britt got me a bottle. Instead of drinking, I poured it into my hand and began slicking back my hair. It took enough water to get my hair under control that people might think I'd just taken a shower. But it was better than the other options of *tacky tourist* or *mad scientist*.

"Ready?" Britt asked.

I drank the rest of the thermos of coffee before giving a thumbs-up. "Ready."

"You didn't ration that?" Britt asked.

My eyebrows rose. "Gables Hall is a big building. I'm sure we can find coffee."

Britt's phone began ringing. "Hang on. It's Sienna."

"Sure thing."

I didn't groan or anything melodramatic, but this could take a while.

Sienna was marrying Britt's brother Paul next month, and there'd been a constant stream of wedding questions. Part of the urgency had to do with them getting married three months after the engagement. But Paul and Sienna were done waiting.

I eyed Britt as she rapid-fired bizarre wedding facts.

Would she want a short engagement?

My hair was almost dry by the time Britt hung up the phone.

"Sorry," Britt said. "There's always a new fire to put out."

"All good," I said—though would Britt consider eloping?

It wasn't until we started walking that I noticed my shirt was backward and I'd somehow put my slacks on without taking off the joggers I'd slept in.

"Hold on."

I did the embarrassing act of removing my light jacket and twisting around my shirt—really wished we weren't in public. I'd leave on the extra pair of pants. It was uncomfortable, but hopefully no one else could tell.

I glanced at Britt. What if she found me too high-maintenance to put up with?

We'd been dating for over a year. She must have an idea of what she'd be signing up for.

It was midmorning. My proposal at the Skydeck was scheduled for the evening. Hopefully, Juniper would be successful. I needed that ring to propose.

Britt noticed my serious face. "We can do this later."

I blinked. It may be a lack of caffeine talking, but I momentarily thought her comment was about getting engaged.

Once I realized she meant our campus investigation, I shook my head. "No. I need to find out if Jacob was plotting with his professor."

Britt hesitated. "If you're sure."

"Yup."

Brittany had directions for Gables Hall on her phone. The walk took us through a maze of old, impressive structures, all a similar shade of tan. There were plenty of trees along the way. But they weren't exactly pretty, since they'd lost their leaves.

Maybe it was the brain fog, but something seemed off. There was barely anyone around, yet I somehow sensed there were plenty of people nearby.

Sensed people? Was I becoming psychic in the Southern Hemisphere?

Ahead of us, a student disappeared through an archway set inside a large building. There came the sound of a distorted voice, like it was amplified through a cheap microphone.

I moved toward the arch.

Thankfully, Britt followed, though I'd neglected to communicate what had caught my attention.

The voice grew louder, yet I couldn't make out the words.

We walked under the archway and found ourselves in a long, vaulted hallway. Sunlight poured in from one side through rows of decorative arches. Past the arches was a courtyard full of people. It wasn't exactly packed, but there was an impressive number of people herded into the area.

Did we belong here? Before I could ask Britt, we were close enough that the voice from the microphone became understandable. "...for Jacob Holt."

Was this a vigil for Jacob?

Call me old-fashioned, but I thought vigils were supposed to happen at night, when candlelight could attempt to fight the darkness creeping in at all sides.

The courtyard fell silent. Most people bowed their heads.

I took Britt's hand and gave it a squeeze.

Since the standard rule for a *moment of silence* is keeping quiet, I couldn't ask what she thought.

I scanned the people. There was a decent amount of the university's dark blue and white colors worn by the gathered students and faculty.

Everyone looked serious, but there were a few faces that appeared genuinely sad.

We carefully moved forward to get a better view of the stage.

Alexa stood beside Jacob's mom and his friend we'd seen with her at the police station. Music began playing—an instrumental version of a song I almost recognized.

No one spoke until the music faded. Then Alexa thanked everyone for coming to grieve as a community...or that's probably what she said.

The sound quality on her mic was bad enough that it was hard to understand.

Next Alexa introduced Jacob's mom, and she took the mic.

I was tempted to leave. I've survived plenty of uncomfortable moments while solving crimes, but listening to a mother give a eulogy about her son was a step too far.

But I was with Brittany, and she wasn't moving.

People began crying as the mom spoke. She didn't mention her personal illness, yet she seemed unsteady, and the sunlight made her heavy makeup more apparent. Jacob's friend stood beside her, ready to catch her if she collapsed.

Britt snuffled and wiped beneath her eyes.

She was crying? I rubbed Britt's back, trying to be comforting.

Personally, I wasn't about to break down. Jacob had stalked me in the airport, taken advantage of my altered mental state, and stolen my passport. His life choices had almost trapped me in the wrong hemisphere.

Jacob's mom sounded less distorted than Alexa, yet it still gave me a headache.

As a private investigator, it must be a good idea to be here. Detectives go to vigils in crime shows all the time. But the reality is a long emotional event that's standing room only.

Wouldn't this be recorded? It would be nicer if Juniper watched it and gave me the highlights.

And honestly, hearing the origin for why Jacob became a snake wrangler was terrifying—it involved a bathtub.

Finally, we were led in a group singing of "Amazing Grace," and the crowd was dismissed.

At last I could talk to Britt. "How sick is Jacob's mom?"

"Very sick."

Is she dying? That question was on the tip of my tongue, yet it was too morbid—even for me.

Britt took my arm. "We should go."

Most people were leaving. Thankfully, the quad was set up with enough exit options that we weren't engulfed by other humans...but there were still too many people.

We'd just started walking when an unexpected figure came into view.

The Bartender leaned against one of the arches with his arms crossed. His eyes were watery, yet he glared at Alexa leaving the stage.

"Morning." Was Britt's smile too bright?

"G'day." The Bartender focused on Britt.

"Hello," I added, when he'd stared at my girlfriend for *too* long.

The Bartender dragged his attention from Britt. But instead of looking at my face, his attention snagged on my pants.

I didn't squirm, but heat crept up my neck. Could he tell I wore joggers underneath my slacks?

"Not used to the cold?" He winked before striding away.

At least The Bartender thought my wearing two pairs of pants was intentional...Though needing extra warmth when it was fifty degrees didn't make me seem tough.

"Don't worry about him." Britt ran a finger along my jaw.

I tried to relax, yet the way The Bartender kept flirting with Britt was irritating.

"The nerve he had to show up." Alexa had walked up without us noticing. She frowned at The Bartender's retreating back. "I begged Jacob to leave that pub."

"Why?" I asked. Based on the little I knew about reptiles, it seemed The Bartender's snakes were getting proper care.

"He ruins wildlife."

"How?" Britt's voice had turned into her calm paramedic one. "Don't all of his snakes have the proper licensing?"

Alexa snorted. "Maybe now. But he's been in prison for smuggling exotic animals. Jacob claimed the pub was legitimate. He was wrong. That man doesn't care about wildlife."

It'd been a while since I'd been around college students. I'd forgotten how fired up they get about ideals.

I'd never had grand goals for improving society. Still, there'd been an adjustment when I stopped being a full-time student and started work as a full-time employee. Alexa got to live in a bubble of ideals before the reality of adult life sank in.

"How do you know he was arrested for smuggling?" Britt asked.

"It's online." Alexa was only too happy to show us the details on her phone.

While I didn't actually know if The Bartender's name was *Dean Williams*, Brittany's nod implied Alexa had the right person.

The Bartender had served close to three years in prison but was released over five years ago without any new offenses.

Am I happy the guy who'd been flirting with Britt had a prison record?

No. Absolutely not. (That would make me very petty.)

Yet, contrary to what Alexa believed, The Bartender's staying out of trouble certainly implied his pub was aboveboard.

The problem was The Bartender hadn't been completely honest. The police had bigger reasons for suspecting him that went beyond owning snakes. He definitely had contacts who could help get a venomous snake to kill Jacob.

As I considered all the possible implications, a woman with strong professor vibes paused and thanked Alexa for her help with the vigil.

Alexa pretended to downplay the compliment, but she wasn't fooling anyone. She loved being praised.

Britt and I tried to break free, yet Alexa caught up to us right as we left the courtyard and rejoined the main campus. "Sorry about that. Professor Campbell was impressed with how smoothly the event ran."

"You helped organize this?" Britt was polite enough to ask.

"It's not that difficult." Alexa waved her hand. "I've had enough practice for different wildlife causes."

All those pamphlets came to mind.

"Remembering the Thylacine," I murmured.

"Yes!" Alexa twisted one of her bulky rings. "I learned about thylacines in elementary school." She held up her hand to show off a ring with the image of an animal etched into the silver. It sort of resembled a skinny hyena with stripes instead of spots. "They're native to Australia but went extinct about a hundred years ago."

Britt nodded. "I've heard about them."

Alexa drew in a breath. "I was so mad when my teacher told me they died out due to hunting and loss of habitat. Thylacines had no one protecting them."

"That's terrible." I tried to put emotion behind my words. But a species dying out a century ago didn't affect me.

As we continued walking, I had the sinking feeling Alexa was also heading to Gables Hall.

Thankfully, Britt's resourceful—and occasionally isn't perfectly polite. Even though her phone clearly showed we needed to stay straight, she took a random turn. "Holt, it's this way." She gave Alexa a quick wave before we made our escape.

The detour added another ten minutes to our walk, but it was worth it to stop the conversation about bizarre animals nobody's heard of.

Gables Hall was larger than the nearby buildings. The entrance had a card reader, but the light was green. I tried the door, and it opened.

"Must be unlocked during school hours," I commented, holding the door for Britt. There were a few wrong turns and some backtracking, but we finally discovered the stairwell that led to the biology floor.

Too bad I was out of coffee. I was about to interview a creepy reptile-ologist and needed all my wits about me...or as many wits as possible for a human wearing two pairs of pants.

On the third floor, the stairwell fire door was shut, but the green light from the card reader showed it was open access.

"This place isn't exactly Fort Knox," I commented.

As we entered a large hallway, what was immediately noticeable was a display case with a variety of taxidermied snakes.

My neck tingled, and I instinctively took Britt's hand.

As much as I hate live snakes, there's something horrendously creepy about taxidermied ones.

I didn't move closer. But I couldn't look away.

"The pygmy python's the newest," a gray-haired man said.

There were people in the hallway, but I hadn't paid them much attention until he started speaking.

"Is that so?" Britt asked, then proceeded to walk to where the man stood by the trophy case of dead things.

Since I hadn't let go of Britt's hand, I was basically dragged along for the ride.

"Yes. Rita was a lovely lady." The man placed a hand on the glass separating him from the snake.

The *snake* was a *lovely lady*?

Nope.

I needed to jump on the next plane to Seattle.

"Holt?"

Britt tugged on my hand and nodded in the man's direction.

Wait.

Given the man's overall reptilian look, I'd say he was our friendly visiting professor. I'd figured out his name last night—I'd even read what his degrees were—yet that information was wiped from my memory.

And he was sad about a dead snake. Would we need to start questioning a suspect while he mourned the passing of a beloved snake?

At least I didn't have to make an introduction. When The Professor turned to give me his attention, his eyes widened. "You're Holt Jacobs."

Who'd have thought Australia would be the place where everyone recognized me?

"That's right. Uh...have we met?"

"Not officially." The Professor did something resembling a laugh, where he flicked his tongue in and out—he needed to spend less time around snakes. "Apologies. I'm not a stalker. Only, a former student had a name similar to yours. We were both quite fascinated when we heard about you." He sighed, and his face took on the sad look it'd had when he'd been staring at the stuffed snake. "Sadly, Jacob's passed on."

"I know," I said dryly. "The police came to my parents' house to notify them of the death. Jacob was found with my passport."

The Professor made a hissing noise and began pacing. "No. No. No. No. He really did it?"

Britt's eyes met mine.

What had Jacob done?

CHAPTER 9

The Professor continued pacing as he muttered incoherently.

"Maybe we should talk in your office?" Britt was employing her professional paramedic voice. She must find his behavior concerning.

"Yes. Yes. How rude," The Professor mumbled. He placed his hand on Britt's back and began leading her down the hallway.

Why were men giving Britt extra attention in Australia? Was it the new continent? Or was there something in the air that warned them there wasn't much time before Britt was permanently off the dating market?

I was afraid The Professor's office would be crowded with a combination of living and taxidermied snakes. Thankfully, the space was snake-free—aside from a rather scary print on the wall of a cobra spitting venom.

The whole space was cluttered.

Hadn't Juniper said he was a *new* professor? How had he accumulated such high heaps of books and papers during his short stay?

"Um, here. Let me." The Professor lifted a stack of folders from the chair opposite his desk and set them on the floor. "Please, sit," he invited Britt, as he took the spot behind the desk.

Since we'd run out of chairs, I stood beside Britt with my hand resting on her shoulder in a casual way—not at all territorial.

The Professor sighed. "I told him not to..."

My jaw ticked. I was dying to ask, *Care to share with the class?* But he seemed the sort who wouldn't handle sarcasm.

Due to my comments being the private kind, Brittany asked, "What did Jacob do?"

"He pretended to be American." The Professor dropped his head into his hands, seemingly defeated.

"How could that work?" I asked. Every Australian I'd been around sounded like they were from Australia.

"Yes, how indeed." The Professor must have been making a rhetorical comment since he knew the answer.

"Professor?" Britt encouraged.

"Right, well, Jacob started telling people his father was American." He stopped talking, like that was all the information we'd need.

"And?" I tried to hide my annoyance.

"Oh, right." The Professor blinked. "Let's see, Jacob claimed he had two passports. That he was both a US and an Australian citizen."

My grip on Britt's shoulder tightened. That whole *double passport thing* sounded like a scam. "That can't be legal."

Britt looked up at me. "Stuff like that happens. A friend from school was both American and Canadian through her parents."

I frowned.

It still sounded fake. But what did I know.

I turned back to The Professor. "What was Jacob hoping to accomplish with his fake dual citizenship?"

The Professor sagged against his chair. "He had contacts who wanted to verify his US nationality. When Jacob heard about your visit, he took it as a sign. With your names being mirrored, he was sure it would work."

"But their birthdays wouldn't match. And their names aren't completely mirrored," Britt pointed out. "Holt's last name is *Jacobs*, not *Jacob*."

The Professor stared intently at Britt. "Trust me. Once you've been a professor as long as I have, you learn that most people don't pay attention to details."

"And just what business was Jacob conducting that required a legitimate US passport?" I asked.

"Well..." The Professor hesitated. He tugged at his collar. "Actually, I'm late for a lecture. If you'll excuse me."

He was lying. I'm one hundred percent certain he was lying. But my brain wasn't working fast enough to give a snappy challenge.

Britt has better manners. She accepted his excuse. "Understood. Thank you for your time."

The Professor knew Jacob's secret but wasn't willing to disclose the information. Was he involved with Jacob's secret project?

The Professor escorted us out of the office, then hurried away. In the hallway, we passed rows of doors, likely a combination of offices, classrooms, and labs.

There was a sign for a restroom beside a door with a card reader.

While I can't say for sure how long it had been since I'd visited a bathroom, I can say the sign reminded me it had been a while.

"Excuse me," I told Britt.

I pulled the door open and stepped inside.

Instead of focusing on my surroundings, I was considering a new question. Should I take off my joggers while in the restroom? It'd be more comfortable, but then I'd need to carry the extra pair of pants—which would look odd.

The door clicked shut behind me, and I couldn't see anything. I waved my arms, expecting motion-activated lights to click on.

But the room stayed dark.

There came a hissing past my right shoulder.

My spine tingled.

This wasn't a bathroom.

Please be in cages. Please be in cages. Please be in cages.

Carefully, I took my phone and turned on the flashlight. I gasped.

It was some sort of miniature rainforest ecosystem. Jungle trees and vines ran throughout the room, and the whole place was hot and uncomfortably muggy.

The hissing came again. I moved the light toward the noise. A pair of beady eyes stared at me.

I would've screamed, but I'd forgotten to breathe. There was no air to make a sound.

A lime-green snake slithered along a branch to get a better look at me.

Was this snake venomous?

Some snakes jump. Was this a breed that could leap long distances?

My options were fight, flight, or freeze.

If memory serves, it's best not to make any sudden movements around wild animals. It meant my lack of movement was a calculated decision...not panic overloading my system.

Right after I'd decided to stay still, a new hiss came from the ground behind me.

I jumped. My phone fell to the ground, blocking the light and making the room almost pitch-black again.

My phone gave a faint glow. Retrieving it would bring me farther into the room, but it would be impossible to get out without light. Gingerly, I moved toward my phone. Could snakes see in the dark, or did they have sonar?

Note to self: *If I survive, start watching animal documentaries.*

My heart was about to hammer out of my chest.

There's a chance my eyes were playing tricks. But once I had my phone and turned the light around the room, thousands of eyes stared back at me.

A snake slithered toward me.

Red stripes touched other stripes. Wasn't there a saying where if red touched one color, the breed was safe, but if it touched a different color, you'd be dead?

However the saying went, I didn't remember it. So there was at least a fifty percent chance it could kill me. The only way I'd know for sure was if it bit me.

Since that outcome was best avoided, I stood completely frozen.

Could snakes tell I was exhibiting nonthreatening behavior?

The red-striped snake stopped by my shoe. It wasn't coiled. It wasn't about to strike. Instead, it rested beside me, like my shoe made good company. I dry heaved, while being careful not to move my feet.

I could barely breathe. Air seemed to get caught in my throat. I was sweating harder than I did on leg day at the gym. It was a miracle I hadn't peed my pants.

My vision began to speckle.

I was in danger of passing out.

Imagining my unconscious body surrounded by hordes of venomous snakes made me dry heave again...Good thing I'd skipped breakfast.

The snake at my feet gave an unhappy hiss but made no move to bite or slither away.

I had to calm down. This was the vacation where I got engaged. Not the trip where I died after wandering into a den of snakes.

But the speckling in my vision grew worse, and there was now a rushing in my ears.

The first problem was that my knees were locked. I bent, while being careful not to disturb my new snake friend.

Then I did something drastic—I took Juniper's advice. Time to see if box breathing could slow down my heart rate.

Breathe in, two, three, four.

Hold, two, three, four.

Exhale, two, three, four.

Hold, two, three, four...

Gradually, the rushing faded and my vision cleared. I was still terrified, but my brain was capable of thinking.

Beyond the snake that was trying to become my shoe's best friend, my biggest problem was that I'd misplaced the exit.

The vines and branches hanging overhead made it feel like I'd teleported into the jungle.

I shone my light in every direction but didn't spot the door. It would've been handy if they'd put up a neon *exit* sign—but that would make escaping too easy.

The room couldn't be very large. I needed to choose a direction and walk until I came to a wall, then follow that until I found the door.

Cautiously, I began shifting my foot away from the snake. I didn't breathe as I created distance between myself and the possibly venomous striped snake.

At first the little guy didn't seem to notice. But when I'd almost broken free of the contact, he moved to again rest against my shoe.

This wasn't working.

Around me, the fake jungle was full of rustlings from other snakes.

I gulped, unfortunately swallowing nothing but air. This couldn't be how I died. I've faced down murderers, almost died from carbon dioxide poisoning, and driven successfully on the wrong side of the road. If I died in here, I'd end up on the news as a dumb tourist who didn't know what an Australian bathroom looked like.

Sweat trickled down my back as I made a second attempt to ease my foot away from the snake.

Obviously, this wasn't the bathroom. There'd been two doors and one card reader. Restrooms don't require special access. The card reader belonged to this jungle.

But why had this door opened? Was the card reader malfunctioning, or had the door not fully sealed shut?

I shouldn't have ended up in here.

Even if the snakes in this jungle *weren't* venomous, a college wouldn't want random people wandering in, messing with the ecosystem.

For now, it didn't matter. I had to escape.

I chose the wall that was my best guess for having the exit.

Could the door with the faulty card reader relate to Jacob's death?

What kind of snake killed him? I tried to remember what it looked like. Had I seen a picture?

My memory was blank.

I needed to leave. My initial rush of adrenaline had faded, and I was starting to crash.

No matter how gently I moved, the striped snake kept shifting to be by my shoe. I'd have to risk it. After a moment's hesitation, I took a massive step away and hurried to a wall.

At first all I could do was sag against it. Reality had distorted until I was living my worst nightmare. Was there any chance this was a dream?

With my free hand, I tried pinching my neck, but my fingers were too numb to get any grip.

Did that make the dream theory a likely option? I could barely feel the phone in my other hand—it was a wonder I hadn't dropped it again.

I'd wasted enough time. I needed to check for the exit.

I leaned heavily against the wall as I walked along it.

No door. I'd chosen wrong.

But that left only three more walls to check—assuming I was in a square room.

I had to move fast. Either the hissing behind me was growing louder, or the rushing in my ears had returned.

I stumbled through a section of branches and hanging vines, trying not to think about the scaly creatures I might brush against. I never lost contact with the wall. Sooner or later there had to be a door. I wasn't going to miss the exit.

The second wall also held no escape.

My body was tingling. All the air was being sucked out of the room. But I had to keep going.

Fainting in the jungle room wasn't an option.

Finally, at the third wall, I caught the beautiful outline of the door. I fell against it, hoping the force would push it open. No such luck.

I tried to grab the handle, yet I'd lost my grip strength. Both hands were too numb. My vision swam, and it seemed like the floor was moving.

I slammed into the door and tried to call "Britt!" but my shout was more of a hoarse whisper. I sagged against the exit, too far gone to come up with new ideas.

There came a scrap of metal, and then I felt the slight give of the latch. It happened too fast for me to react. I tumbled through the door, nearly tackling Brittany.

"Close it. Close it. Close it," I panted. Someplace far away was the click of a door. But I didn't stop repeating "Close it."

I was on my hands and knees. Britt was touching my face. She said something, but I couldn't hear. The rushing intensified, and I fainted.

CHAPTER 10

I don't recommend passing out in the hallway of a college building.

When my eyes blinked open, a group of curious students had gathered just past Britt.

"That must've been some party," one guy said.

Another person shushed him. "See all that sweat? It must be a medical condition."

I groaned and closed my eyes. Could I be lucky enough to faint again?

"What happened?" This voice held the authority of a grown man.

Britt squeezed my hand. "He fainted."

"Is that...? Was he...?" The man cleared his throat. "All right, students. That's enough. Get back to class. And, Oliver, delete that recording."

Recording? I was half-tempted to sit up and confirm that the footage got destroyed. But I couldn't move. My vision refused to fully focus, and my body was cold and shaky.

"Did he, uhh...?" The Professor's face swam into view.

"Wander into your snake room?" My voice was all gravel. "Yes, I did."

"He's fine," The Professor said loudly to a pair of students walking past.

"Why doesn't that door lock?" My words were almost slurred. I was close to fainting again.

"There's a couch in my office," The Professor said. "He can recover there."

"Come on." Britt leaned down and wrapped my arm over her shoulder. "Time to go."

I was trembling, and it took Britt and The Professor's help to move me back to his office. When we made it inside, The Professor let go of me. I continued to lean heavily against Brittany as he began unburying a couch that had previously disappeared beneath a heap of books and documents.

The office door suddenly flew open.

Alexa appeared, framed perfectly in the doorway. "You liar!" she yelled at The Professor, seemingly unaware of me or Britt.

He dropped a folder at her entrance, but when The Professor spoke, his voice was controlled. "Please, Alexa. This isn't the time."

Alexa's eyebrows shot up. "Are you denying that an American tourist wandered into the snake room?"

I tried to comment, but the only sound I made was a strange gurgling.

The noise was enough to gain Alexa's attention. "Holt? What are...? Were you the...?"

At this point the couch was empty enough for Britt to help me flop across the cushions.

"I'll get water." Britt pressed a kiss to my damp forehead before leaving me alone with two people midargument.

"I told you what Jacob was doing." Alexa took a menacing step closer to The Professor. "You said you'd handle it."

"Well..." The Professor kept clenching and unclenching his hands. "I tried. Or I thought I did, but..."

Someone needed to explain to me what was going on. But when I was finally able to string words into sentences, I surprised myself by asking, "Were there venomous snakes in there?"

The Professor said, "No," right as Alexa said, "Yes."

Instead of clarifying, they glared at each other.

"You promised," Alexa stated, then stormed out of the room—colliding with Britt as she returned with a plastic cup of water.

Water sloshed first on Britt and then on Alexa before splattering to the floor.

A shocked silence followed the mishap. Britt sent me a questioning glance, like I'd be able to explain what was going on.

Alexa pressed her lips together like she was trying really hard not to yell.

It was The Professor who broke the tension. "I have paper towels." He marched over to a file cabinet and began opening random drawers until a wad of crumpled paper towels materialized. "Here. Get yourselves cleaned up while I wipe up the floor."

Britt gladly accepted the offer, yet from how Alexa's frown intensified, it was clear she was tempted to refuse his help. In the end, she accepted the paper towels and began drying off her clothes. "Sorry," she mumbled to Britt. "I wasn't expecting you."

Britt waved her off. "Don't worry about it. No damage done."

"Thanks," Alexa said, but her attention had wandered to where I lay on the couch. "I'll get more water."

She left before Britt could tell her not to bother.

Britt looked down to where The Professor was still on his hands and knees wiping up the final drips. "Time to explain what's going on." Her voice held the authority she must occasionally employ as a paramedic.

I couldn't help smiling. It was sexy when Britt got a little bossy.

But The Professor didn't crack. He stood up slowly and shook his head. "There's nothing to tell."

I snorted. "Nothing? A private jungle full of snakes with a door that doesn't lock isn't worth mentioning?"

Alexa reappeared in the doorway carrying a disposable water bottle. "Should I tell them?"

Alexa, Britt, and I were all in different spots around the room. The Professor had no safe place to look.

With him stuck in indecision, Alexa walked toward me with the water bottle—this was less likely to spill than the cup. But she had to pass The Professor to reach me. He took the water and began drinking greedily.

I gave a surprised croak. How hard was it to get a drink?

When the bottle was half-empty, The Professor let out a contented sigh and moved to his desk chair. "Really, there's not much to say." He sounded like my lawyer buddy Darren when he was skirting the truth.

"Fine." Alexa tilted her chin defiantly. "While I was dating Jacob, I thought he was interested in me. Since his passing, I discovered he was using me to get access to Gables Hall."

The Professor tried to act uninterested as he typed on his keyboard. But given that his monitors were off, he wasn't being productive.

"How hard is it to get a teaching visa?" Britt asked the room. "There must be certain requirements guaranteeing good behavior."

"Sure," I agreed. "Imagine the hassle if the university found out a visiting professor was under investigation."

"At a certain point, the uni might decide it was best to send the professor home instead of dealing with the fallout," Alexa added.

The Professor clawed at his shirt collar. His face had turned rather blotchy. He gulped down the rest of the water.

We all waited as he stared at the floor.

"Jacob had fascinating ideas," The Professor admitted. "He wasn't a student in my classes, but we started talking during office hours and..."

"And?" My voice had an edge to it. This guy's behavior was really starting to irritate me.

His nostrils flared. "It's all complex, scientific stuff. Wouldn't want to overwhelm you."

I snorted. "Complex ideas are fine. It's rooms full of snakes I find overwhelming."

The Professor winced. "Like I said, Jacob wasn't actually my student. He had to complete prerequisites before he could be eligible for my classes."

Britt cleared her throat, signaling he needed to get to the point.

"However," The Professor added, possibly scared of my girlfriend, "Jacob wanted to be involved. I caught him in the snake room once. I tried to be furious, but he was too passionate about my work to stay mad."

"Did he tell you how he got inside?"

The Professor shrugged, apparently unconcerned with the gap in security. "He mentioned a program he bought that caused card readers to malfunction."

"You knew?" I struggled to sit up, my muscles still tingly.

The Professor's ears turned a truly impressive shade of pink. "I didn't realize Jacob would actually steal our only—" He abruptly stopped talking.

I don't know exactly what Jacob stole, but presumably it was a rare snake.

Alexa began pacing around the office, apparently too worked up to speak.

"And you didn't realize the card reader was completely disabled until Holt got trapped inside?" Britt clarified.

"I, uh...not exactly. I knew for a couple of days." The Professor picked up the plastic water bottle before realizing it was empty and setting it back down. "Jacob's death. The venom made me think...Anyway, the police informed me he was bitten by a rough-scaled-midnight snake. They're almost extinct. But the university has..." He sighed. "Well, I checked the door to the snake room. Sure enough, it was unlocked even though the red light was blinking."

"You knew since Jacob died?" I asked. "Then why wasn't it fixed?"

He shrugged. "Maintenance couldn't figure out how to override what Jacob had done. They ordered a replacement and will install it once the shipment arrives."

"But what was Jacob doing with the rough-scaled-midnight snake?" Britt asked.

"And what does that have to do with my passport?"

"The rough-scaled-midnight snake?" The Professor turned his gaze away. "They're native to Australia. Aside from the university, the remaining snakes are found on protected land." He sighed. "That snake is the reason I applied to be a visiting professor at the University of Melbourne."

Was he serious? This man flew halfway across the world because he wanted to be closer to a specific breed of snake?

"What's so special about the midnight snake?" I didn't bother hiding my skepticism.

The Professor frowned at me. Like I was weird since I wasn't saying, *Yes, it makes perfect sense to switch continents to be closer to a reptile.*

"Please tell us." Britt smiled expectantly.

The Professor responded better to friendliness. His eyes lit up with her question. "The rough-scaled-midnight snake is a subspecies of the rough-scaled snake. Studies on the rough-scaled-midnight snake are rare due to how few there are. But it's thought the venom might be utilized for cancer treatments."

My stomach gurgled. Partially from a lack of food, but also from turning snake venom into a prescription.

"Snake venom is already used in some treatments." Alexa ran a finger along her ring. "But this breed is in danger of becoming extinct."

I shared a look with Britt. In general, I'd stopped checking product ingredients after I learned whale vomit is used in expensive perfume.

"What did Jacob want with the snake?" I asked. If The Professor was willing to move to Australia for the honor of studying the breed, I'm guessing Jacob's motives were less pure.

"There was...sort of a bounty for that snake."

"Come off it." Alexa's hands balled into fists. "There's a pharmaceutical company in the US that's willing to spend millions for the honor of having a rough-scaled-midnight snake in their lab."

"Hold on." Britt's eyes narrowed. "Neither Australia nor the US is going to let you travel with a deadly snake."

"That's correct," The Professor agreed. "Yet the pharmaceutical company wasn't concerned with *how* they got the snake. If Jacob proved he had the snake, I'm sure they'd figure out a plan to retrieve it."

"And Jacob saw the opportunity to steal the snake?" Britt asked.

The Professor held his hands up. "I didn't think he'd really do it. Finding out about *Holt Jacobs's* visit to Melbourne must've felt like a sign."

I frowned. "It can't be easy for US citizens to fly into America with a snake on the plane."

"Right. It's not easy. Neither country encourages the transportation of snakes." The Professor sighed, looking tired. "But Jacob had friends with security clearances that only applied to US citizens."

Okay.

Jacob had planned to disappear into America before he got murdered by a venomous snake, which he'd stolen while having my passport in his possession.

Who'd kill him? And what had they done with the endangered snake?

Could Jacob have met up with a partner and they'd taken his life instead of sharing the money?

Maybe. But it seemed more likely his partners were in the US.

A different option was that someone wanted to stop Jacob badly enough, they were willing to kill him. It gave us a potential *why*.

We already knew the *how*: death caused by snake bite.

We were left with *who*. And currently I shared a room with two very good suspects...

Chapter 11

As we left The Professor's office, Britt paused in the hallway. There was a giant poster of two seemingly identical snakes. "This could be helpful," she said. "It's a comparison between a rough-scaled snake and the midnight subspecies."

I glanced at the writing. Basically, the rough-scaled-midnight snake was the same—except that its venom had an added compound making it much more lethal.

The only visible difference between the two was that rough-scaled-midnight snakes had dark blue pupils instead of black pupils like regular rough-scaled snakes.

"Why not take a picture?" Britt suggested.

"Good idea." She was right. It might come in handy.

But Britt didn't get her phone. She nodded toward me. I snapped a quick shot.

"Have you looked at your photos from the trip?" Britt asked.

"No." I slipped my phone back into my pocket. "Anything important is on Mom's phone."

I headed straight for the stairs. It was time to escape the creepy third floor. But Britt tugged at my arm. She nodded toward a young man who stood by the trophy case of taxidermied snakes with his head bowed.

What? I mouthed at Britt.

Police station, she mouthed back.

Huh?

I reexamined the man. He was the guy with Jacob's mom by the elevators and from the vigil. I'm not the best at recognizing faces under normal circumstances. And if wearing two pairs of pants is any indicator, I wasn't at my peak mentally.

Britt approached and employed her empathetic paramedic voice. "Is there someone I can call?"

The guy jumped. "Have we met?"

"Not really," Britt said. "We saw you at the police station yesterday."

"You know about Jacob?" he asked.

We nodded.

"I can't believe this happened," the young guy said. "His mom's really sick. Who would take her son away?"

Good thing Britt was there. She was able to handle all the feeling parts of the conversation.

It was taking all my mental energy to put two and two together.

Not only was Jacob's mom sick, but a pharmaceutical company wanted a rough-scaled-midnight snake for cancer research.

Had Jacob stolen the snake, hoping they'd find a miracle cure for his mom? His murder wasn't about money or greed. All he'd wanted was his mom to get better.

My eyes started watering.

We needed to leave. Being around Jacob's friend was making my allergies flare up...and I felt a strange urge to hug my mom.

After Britt had finished comforting Jacob's friend, we left the third floor. We checked Mom's office. The door was unlocked, but she was gone. There was a note saying she was giving a lecture.

Since we couldn't hang out with Mom, Britt got us a car, and we took the ride back to my parents' place.

I'm not exactly proud of this, but I ate, showered, and then took a nap. The terror I'd experienced in the snake room had left me horribly drained.

I woke up to my phone vibrating. Juniper's name flashed across the screen. "Hello?" I growled.

"Were you sleeping?" Juniper was too perky. Was she chugging energy drinks? "If I can't sleep, you can't sleep."

I rolled onto my back. "Noted. Thanks for calling."

My thumb was poised to hang up when Juniper yelled, "Wait!"

My finger froze.

"Is Brittany there?"

I looked around the basement to make sure. "No. I'm alone."

"Super." Juniper dropped her voice to *top-secret* volume. "I called the airports, double-checked with the airline, and tried a couple of other places. None of them has any record of your ring."

I squeezed my eyes shut. I'm not big on *the universe sending cosmic signs*, yet losing a legacy engagement ring days before the proposal was about as bad an omen as I could get.

"Holt?" my sister called.

"It's a sign," I mumbled, unwilling to open my eyes.

"Nope."

Did Juniper think that one word could fix everything?

Juniper should've stopped there, but she felt the need to explain further. "The only thing misplacing Grandma's old ring shows is that you're meant to buy Britt a *real* ring that was made in this century."

I imagined going into a fancy showroom, walking past display cases of glittering diamonds, and my stomach clenched. Sure, I could afford a ring that would make Juniper jealous, yet that was all wrong for Britt.

She'd hate to wear anything gaudy and was far too practical to want thousands of dollars on her finger.

"Holt?" Juniper asked.

"I'm thinking."

"If you don't have the ring in Australia and didn't forget it at your apartment, it must be lost."

"I know," I said through gritted teeth. I'd hoped Jacob had taken the ring when he'd taken the passport, yet that possibility was becoming highly unlikely.

"It's getting late," Juniper said. "Shouldn't you get ready for your appointment at the Skydeck?"

She was right. If I was going to the Skydeck, I needed to start moving.

Could I propose without the ring? Plenty of men had done it, yet that wasn't right.

Britt had already been engaged. From the little I'd heard about Jeremy, he must've planned quite an elaborate stage for popping the question. It'd be a rough comparison if I couldn't figure out how to have one small rock when I got down on one knee.

There came a creak on the stairs. "Quiet," I whispered before Juniper said another word about engagement rings.

The light knock on the door, followed by the handle slowly opening, had to be Britt. I was grinning even before she came into view.

"Hey," she said almost shyly. "I heard talking and wanted to make sure you were okay."

"It's Juniper," I said, holding up the phone.

"Helloooo!" my sister called.

Britt waved, but her attention was on me. "You told me there was a surprise this afternoon?"

"Yeah," I said. "Let me change, and then I'll head up."

Britt glanced from me to Juniper. "Okay."

Once Britt left, Juniper held up her hand and wiggled her ring finger. I groaned and flopped back on the bed. How did I get into this mess?

But I couldn't propose without Grandma's ruby.

"Can you call the Skydeck?" I asked.

"Why?"

I didn't want to answer. But I had to.

At the point where I'd already paid for five minutes of privacy on the Skydeck, it'd be a shame to waste it.

"We'll go to the Skydeck, but I'm...not proposing."

Juniper shook her head. "Holt, that's—"

"I need the ring."

She gave a little-sister sigh. Code for, *You're being impossible.*

"Juniper, I gotta go. Will you tell them there's no proposal?"

"Fine. I'll call the Skydeck. But this is a mistake."

"Thanks, sis," I muttered before hanging up.

I'd planned on wearing a special suit, but I couldn't overdress since I was postponing the proposal. Instead of a button-up shirt and a suit jacket, I put on a polo.

When I went upstairs, Britt was waiting in the living room with my parents. Dad was reading a book, while Mom was on her laptop.

"Everyone ready?" I asked.

"For...?" Mom asked.

"The surprise," I said. "Remember I asked you to keep the schedule clear?"

"That included us?" Dad asked.

"Of course it did."

I was gaslighting the people closest to me. But if Britt and I went to the Skydeck alone, there'd be no explaining why I *didn't* propose. If my parents were there...Well, no one wants to get engaged with their mommy and daddy watching.

"Your parents are coming?" Britt tilted her head quizzically.

"Sure they are." I tried not to look guilty. "Mom's not the only one who can plan family outings."

"Okay." Britt smoothed down the dress she'd changed into. She looked extra nice—like she'd expected engagement photos.

I tugged at my collar. Was the room getting hotter?

My parents and Britt all shared confused looks. Everyone must've correctly assumed I'd planned on popping the question this evening. My current behavior was an unexpected curveball.

"Holt..." Brittany hesitated. "Should we talk?"

"We can talk in the car. We're running late."

When we got to the Skydeck, the staff gave me a few pitying looks. *What had Juniper told them?* Aside from their glances, it was nothing but professional courtesy as we were escorted to the elevator for our private few minutes on the Skydeck.

"Wow," Britt breathed, as the elevator doors opened onto the eighty-eighth floor.

I'd seen videos taken from the Skydeck, but those didn't do it justice. Buildings and sky surrounded us—it was quite a view. I wrapped my arm around her, hating how *almost perfect* wasn't good enough for a proposal.

We walked to the closest window, taking in the sight of the city stretching out around us.

"How about a photo?" Britt asked. "Let's use your phone."

"I can take it," Mom offered.

"No!" Britt tried to laugh. "I want a selfie on Holt's phone."

Huh?

I glanced at Mom. Did Mom know what was going on?

Mom winked before walking away.

Apparently, Britt didn't want to share our moment with anyone.

"Get over here." I pulled Britt close, then opened my camera, and we posed for a few shots. I tried to be charming and romantic, but I was acting. I hated this.

Britt took the phone and began scrolling through the images. She reached a video. "What's this?"

I frowned. "No idea. Looks like I filmed it on the plane."

"Should we watch it?" she asked.

"Absolutely not." I shuddered. "I don't need to watch myself sleep-talk."

"Holt, it's—"

"Not now."

"Okay." Britt sighed. I got the feeling she was disappointed—but that made two of us.

I ran my hand along her shoulder, her hair brushing through my fingers. Britt must know that even if I wasn't proposing on the Skydeck, I still wanted to marry her.

"Quite a view," I said.

Britt leaned into me. "This reminds me of our date at the Space Needle."

"Except this building is about twice as high," I said.

"And they probably don't give you a free T-shirt if you take the stairs down."

"I would have bought you a T-shirt," I growled—we were reliving a favorite argument.

Britt giggled. "It wouldn't be the same."

"Yeah, we wouldn't have blisters. You were in heels, and I had on dress shoes."

"Those blisters were battle scars," Britt said.

I laughed.

But that lightness quickly vanished.

A tightness grew in my chest, and my throat felt swollen. Too much tension was swirling inside me.

I needed to calm down.

I had to put distance between me and Britt as fast as possible.

After a quick kiss, I slipped away.

Once I'd made an escape, Mom joined Britt, and together they pointed excitedly at different views.

Dad sat with *The Silver Chair* open in his lap. He'd examine the view, then read a few lines from his current Narnia book, before looking back out the window.

This was what the trip was supposed to be. Mom bringing us to cool locations and me sitting next to Dad when we got tired of adventuring. Instead, the trip had the makings of a spy thriller, complete with stolen passports, missing jewels, and pharmaceutical espionage.

Dad gave a slight chuckle at something in his book. For a moment I was jealous. Dad experienced thousands of lives through book pages, while I was stuck stressed out with the mess I'd created.

"What did you think when the police notified you of my death?"

Dad glanced up from the book. When he saw my face, he fully closed it. "I knew you were in the kitchen," he said. "Still...for a moment that aching worry that a parent never gets rid of came bubbling up. It was less than a second, but I was terrified they were right."

I cleared my throat. Why had I asked?

"And," Dad continued, "I worried they somehow got the names wrong and your mom was..." Dad couldn't even finish that sentence.

I shook my head. "This whole trip's been surreal."

"It's the jet lag."

That surprised a laugh out of me. "True."

I opened my phone's camera roll. There weren't many photos from Australia. Aside from the snake poster, they all included Britt. But the pictures seemed unreal, like snapshots of dreams.

My finger hovered over the video of the two of us on the airplane—who knew what half-asleep me thought was worthwhile content. Maybe I'd decided to become a social media influencer. But with the day I was having, I wasn't ready to watch another embarrassing moment.

Instead, I tapped on the poster detailing rough-scaled snakes. I zoomed in on the photo.

Dad leaned over to see my phone. "Is that a keelback snake?"

"No."

"Really?" Dad looked closer at the image. "One of my coworkers showed me photos of a keelback he caught in his yard. It looked just like that."

Obviously, Dad was wrong. The image we were looking at was from the biology wing of a university. I had no doubt this was a rough-scaled snake.

But that didn't make sense. Dad rarely made mistakes. If he thought the snakes looked alike, there had to be an explanation.

"This is a rough-scaled snake." I pointed to the name at the top of the poster. "Maybe your coworker was confused about the breed that was in his yard."

"Doubtful." Dad leaned forward, tracking a bird flying between the skyscrapers. "Professor Rhys specializes in snakes."

Professor Rhys? Wasn't he The Professor?

"You know him?"

Dad raised a surprised eyebrow. "*You* know him?"

I wasn't prepared to explain the snake den and passing out. Instead, I shrugged. "Saw him on campus."

Dad waited. He could tell there was more. But when I stayed silent, he explained. "I met Professor Rhys at a faculty party. He talked a lot about his wife."

"Sure," I agreed automatically. Did I know he was married? Had The Professor worn a wedding band? "Actually, what about his wife?"

"She died last year." Dad cleared his throat. "Cancer."

My eyebrows shot up.

Was it possible he wasn't just a creepy reptile-ologist? Was he searching for cures to the disease that had stolen his wife?

That would explain why The Professor had been willing to change continents. He wanted to study the rough-scaled-midnight snake to save lives.

It didn't give a clear solution to who killed Jacob, yet we must be getting close.

I was about to ask if Dad knew anything more about The Professor, but Dad was reading the details about rough-scaled snakes.

Dad had a very professorial frown as he considered the new information. That he'd incorrectly assumed a rough-scaled snake was a different breed had to be another clue.

"You're positive he called the snake a *keelback*?"

"Yes." Dad grinned. "Hard to forget such a perfectly Australian name for a snake."

I shook my head. But Dad was right. It would be easy to make jokes like, *Seen any keelbacks at the outback?*

I did a quick online search to get details on keelback snakes. They were also native to Australia but were nonvenomous.

While Dad was wrong about the poster snake being a keelback, the mistake was understandable. They looked an awful lot like rough-scaled snakes.

Based on the internet, the main difference was that keelbacks were brown with almost a black checkerboard pattern, while rough-scaled snakes were brown with dark blotches.

Keelbacks also have *loreal scales.* Which was a fancy way of saying there was an extra scale between their eyes and nose...but who's getting close enough to a snake to check for an extra scale?

"Did you know snakes are believed to have mystical properties?" Dad asked. "It depends on the culture. But throughout history, they're heroes, villains, or gods."

I wasn't sure how to respond to Dad's comment.

In the end, I stared at my phone even as the screen grew dim before turning black.

How common was the keelback snake? Was it a breed The Bartender would have at his pub? If so, where better to hide a rough-scaled-midnight snake than with its nonvenomous lookalikes?

Last night, I'd suggested Jacob had hidden a venomous snake at the Reptile Pub. I'd been on the right track but had suggested the wrong person. What if Jacob's killer had hidden the snake?

"Fancy a drink?" I asked.

Dad nodded. "I know just the place."

Since we were eighty-eight floors up, we couldn't sneak out the back.

I approached Mom and Britt. Before I could suggest going to the Reptile Pub, I was tasked with choosing my favorite bridge.

"Um, that one." I pointed at the first bridge I spotted.

Mom and Britt shared a look.

I was beyond caring if I was being rude. "Can we go?"

"Sure." The way Britt stood, with her hair falling around her shoulders, made me forget to breathe.

It didn't matter that I'd lost the ring. I wasn't leaving Australia without asking Britt to be my wife. (Though imagine how awkward the flight would be if she said no.)

"What's on your mind?" Britt asked once she caught me staring.

"Nothing." I shrugged. "Jet lag."

Not exactly the truth, but I wasn't going to propose in front of my parents, which meant we'd be getting engaged somewhere other than the Melbourne Skydeck.

I debated whether or not Mom would approve of going on a snake hunt at the Reptile Pub. Before I'd decided, Dad told her, and she was surprisingly willing to change her plans.

"Do they have a supper menu?" Mom asked on the walk to the car.

I groaned.

It's dreadful setting foot in that building. But eating? With a deep freezer of dead mice a few yards away?

My face must've turned gray, because Britt whispered, "We don't need to eat there."

It wasn't until Dad parked and we all stared at the Reptile Pub that Brittany said, "Okay, game plan."

"Right." I reopened the snake comparisons on my phone. "The keelback snake has an extra scale between its nose and eyes, and its scales are more of a checkerboard pattern. We're looking for a rough-scaled-midnight snake, which would have a dark blue pupil, and its markings would be blotchier."

I showed everyone photos.

My college professor parents shared a nervous look, like they'd forgotten to study for finals week.

"Actually, I don't know much about snakes," Mom confessed—like at thirty-one I still expected my parents to know everything.

"And just how secure are these snake enclosures?" Dad asked.

Britt's eyes sparkled. "Is everyone in the Jacobs family afraid of snakes?"

"Only the venomous ones," Dad said.

"And the constrictors," Mom added.

Britt's eyebrows rose skeptically. "That true?"

I shrugged. "As shown by keelbacks impersonating rough-scaled snakes, it's best to treat every snake like it's venomous."

Dad murmured his agreement, but Mom was already out of the car. "Coming?" she called.

I sighed. Ready or not, we were about to start a snake hunt.

Inside the bar, the back two tables were packed with students bent over laptops. I shuddered. Why study in such a horrifying place?

The Bartender's eyebrows shot up when we paraded in. Wordlessly, he began pouring four beers.

"Why don't you show me the snakes?" Mom spoke unnaturally loudly as she did strange things with her eyes.

Was she trying to act normal?

"I, too, would like to examine the snakes." Dad sounded like he was performing Shakespeare.

A headache began forming between my temples. Future reference, leave the parents at home during undercover sleuthing missions.

Have I mentioned there's a shocking number of snakes in the bar?

The place was nothing but cages and heat lamps. Once we had our beer, we began examining each enclosure.

Each of us had our own system.

Dad read the breed from the label beside the cage, then searched the type on his phone to verify the snake matched its breed.

I was too jumpy to be methodical. Instead, I walked the area scanning for potential matches.

We hadn't been looking very long when The Bartender asked, "Never seen a snake in America?" It almost sounded like a joke, yet his arms were crossed and he was watching us.

I tried not to be jealous when Britt tossed her hair over her shoulder. "Holt's parents insisted we show them your bar. We haven't stopped talking about it. You've created something very special."

The Bartender grunted. He wasn't quite convinced, yet Britt's charm offensive worked enough that he stopped staring and began arranging glasses.

We resumed searching.

There were at least three cages that held keelbacks. I spent extra time analyzing them. As best I could tell, the scales were the checkerboard pattern of the nonvenomous keelbacks. And none of them had dark blue pupils.

Still, the problem with snake cages is that they have a thick layer of bedding for snakes to burrow in and some form of enclosure for the snake to hide in.

The snakes I spotted checked the correct nonvenomous boxes, but could our missing rough-scaled-midnight snake be burrowed underground?

"Did you see this?" Britt called. She stood by the first enclosure I'd found with the keelback breed.

There'd only been one snake in the cage, and it'd been hard to spot. An inch or two of its tail was visible through foliage by a fake rock formation. The rest of the twenty-inch snake must've been coiled up inside.

"I checked the pattern," I said. "Was there something else?"

Britt tilted her head. "Does it look off?"

I tried to give the snake as much attention as Britt had, but I didn't know what I was looking for.

There were at least two snake holes in the bedding.

Maybe a snake was hiding below, but it's not like Britt had x-ray vision. What had her worried?

"You see its tail?" she asked.

"Yeah, I checked it out." I shrugged. "This should be a keelback snake."

"That's right," Britt agreed. "But is it dead?"

Dead?

I'll be the first to admit I'm not a reptile expert, but how could Britt tell from an inch of tail if the scaly creature was dead?

"I see what you mean." Mom had joined us and was examining the small portion of the snake.

I didn't see anything concerning, but the women in my life were sure the snake was dead.

Should we ask The Bartender if the snake was alive?

Personally, I didn't want to initiate a conversation with the man. But if Britt asked, he'd flirt with her. I was tempted to have Mom ask, but I was about to propose. I needed to show I'm independent...Plus, Mom was horrible at acting normal.

Once I reached the bar, I froze up. The Bartender had a long gold and black snake wrapped across his shoulders.

Before this trip I hadn't considered how utterly horrifying snakes were. Thankfully, my life in Seattle has been snake-free.

"Refill?" The Bartender asked.

"Uh, no." My beer was half-full. "Actually, we were wondering if one of your snakes is dead."

The Bartender's head shot up. When he saw the cage my family was crowded around, he frowned. "Don't worry. Billie's fine."

My immediate follow-up question was *Why name a snake Billie?* But I kept that to myself. "You're sure?" The gold and black snake moved to stare at me. I took a step back. "Uh, my girlfriend's pretty convinced it's dead."

Nothing from The Bartender.

"She's a paramedic."

The Bartender crossed his arms. "I know my snakes. It's not dead. Now, if there's nothing else..." He nodded toward the exit.

Right.

It was time to go.

We'd spent plenty of time examining the cages. None of us had spotted the missing rough-scaled-midnight snake.

I paid for our drinks before returning to my family. "Let's go."

"But what about...?" Mom trailed off when I gave her a look. Her posture changed, and she loudly announced, "We ought to be going."

Her acting wouldn't have been so bad if Dad hadn't said "Righto" on his way out. Was Dad's undercover persona British?

I wanted to rip out my hair. I'm not saying I'd make a great spy, but at least I'm better at secret missions than my parents.

Britt waited until we were halfway to the car before asking, "What was that all about?"

"I asked The Bartender if the snake was dead. He said no and suggested we leave."

"Great Scott!" Dad exclaimed—apparently still in character.

"He's lying," Mom said.

"Yes," Britt agreed. "But why lie about a dead snake?"

Why indeed?

CHAPTER 12

Back at the house, Mom immediately disappeared into the kitchen. Since Britt liked to be useful, she volunteered to help—though her lack of cooking skills made her best suited for tasks like peeling potatoes and washing dishes.

I slunk down to the basement to give Juniper a call. She was the only person who knew the messed-up details of my botched proposal.

"It was awful," I said before her video loaded.

I should've waited.

Instead of Juniper, my brother in-law Jude answered.

"Holt," he greeted.

All I did was nod. Was I rude for never wondering where Juniper's husband was? We'd been talking at all hours of the night, and she'd never mentioned him.

"Good to see you." That wasn't technically true, but it sounded polite. "Uhh, where's Juniper?"

"She's...resting." Jude flipped the camera to show my sister curled up on the couch with her head in his lap.

"I see."

An awkward pause followed. I wasn't ready to unburden myself to my reserved brother-in-law.

Why had he answered the call? Jude barely spoke.

He must've read my mind.

"Juniper needed a nap, but was worried she'd miss you," Jude said. "I promised to answer if you called."

"Did she expect you to wake her up?"

Jude smirked. "She was too tired to ask me. I take it there was no engagement?"

"Right." I wasn't shocked that Juniper had told her husband about my Australian mishaps, but that didn't make it any less humiliating. I needed to take the focus off me. "Are you a fan of her *insomnia challenge*?"

"Eh." Jude leaned back, highlighting the shadows beneath his eyes. "I've been traveling more than normal. The longer I'm gone, the more—*projects*—she thinks up."

My sister made a noise in her sleep.

"I'd better go," he said. "I'll let Juniper know you called."

"Thanks."

"Take care," he offered as the screen went black.

I stared at the phone for a moment.

I'd never really considered how well they worked as a couple. Jude was the silent type and had a top-secret job, while Juniper was bubbly and made her living on social media. On paper they didn't make sense, yet they enjoyed sharing their lives.

Did Britt and I make sense on paper?

I don't know.

Britt's mom would say we didn't.

What did any of that matter? My life was better with Brittany, and she seemed to feel the same way about me.

I went back upstairs. It was bad enough I'd let Britt down at the Skydeck. I shouldn't spend the evening moping in the basement.

Dad caught me in the hallway before I got to the kitchen. He clapped a hand on my shoulder. "Come with me to the porch."

It was more command than request, but since it was Dad, I had no problem joining him on the patio furniture.

At first we sat in silence. Finally, Dad sighed and leaned toward me. The sincerity in his eyes clued me in that this was a conversation I'd rather avoid.

"You've been distracted the whole vacation," Dad said.

I shrugged. "Earlier you thought it was jet lag."

"Come on, Holt," he said dryly. "I've been your dad a long time. Your mom and I assumed when you wanted this afternoon blocked off so..." But Dad couldn't finish the sentence.

He'd stayed silent far too long.

He wasn't going to ask, *Why didn't you propose?*

I lowered my head into my hands. "This trip hasn't gone according to plan."

"I'll bet." Dad's eyes sparkled. "I convinced your mom to be more relaxed this visit. You and Britt didn't need a strict schedule. Now, instead of seeing the sights of Melbourne, you've spent your time at a bar, in a police station, and on a college campus."

We'd also gone to the Melbourne Museum and the Skydeck, but I got Dad's point. "Sorry I've been off. Must be too many snakes."

This time Dad didn't comment. His kind eyes watched and waited. He wouldn't push any farther than he already had, yet he was worried.

I raked a hand through my hair. I hated confessing I'd lost Grandma's ring. But the truth would come out sooner or later. Might as well tell Dad now, when he was expecting bad news.

"I'd planned on proposing to Britt on the Skydeck." I paused, expecting Dad to react, but he stayed silent. My proposal plans weren't a startling revelation. "Umm...anyway, I got Grandma's ring from Casey. But I lost it somewhere between LA and Melbourne."

"The ring's gone?" Pain clouded Dad's eyes, but he blinked it away. "That's what's got you worried?"

"That and the dead body," I muttered.

Dad leaned back. He squeezed his eyes shut for a moment before he smiled. "Did you know your grandfather lost his wedding ring every couple of years?"

I raised an eyebrow. That couldn't be right.

"It's true. He'd take his ring off while working on a project and forget where he put it. Your grandma started having a spare ring or two ready as replacements." The sadness was back in Dad's eyes, and this time he didn't try to hide it. "It's too bad your Grandma's ring disappeared, but it's a family tradition to lose rings. They were married for fifty-seven years, so it must be good luck."

I raised an eyebrow. "That's not how luck works."

"Are you sure?"

I gave a frustrated laugh. It's hard to argue about luck.

"I keep hoping it'll turn up," I admitted. "But I've looked everywhere. I've torn Jacob's life apart. Juniper's called every transportation service I used. And I'm positive I didn't leave it at my apartment."

"Accidents happen" was all Dad said.

Why was he being philosophical? How could he be calm when I lost his mother's ring?

"Doesn't it seem like misplacing the ring might be uh, a...bad omen?"

Dad's eyes sharpened. "Absolutely not. You and Britt belong together." He clapped my shoulder. "Like I said, losing the ring is actually good luck."

I huffed out a breath, and we both sat in silence. "Should I still propose in Australia?"

"Probably."

"Should I sneak out and buy a new ring?"

"Maybe."

Good talk, Dad.

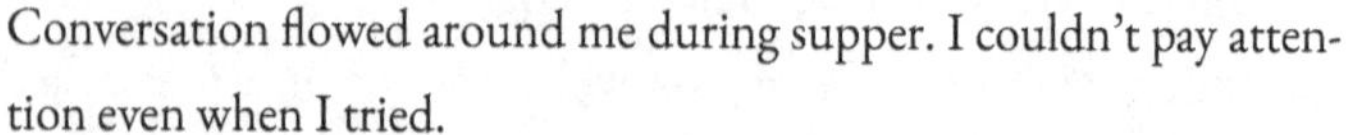

Conversation flowed around me during supper. I couldn't pay attention even when I tried.

Jacob had known I would be arriving in Melbourne because Mom worked with his girlfriend. He was smuggling a rare snake into the US and needed an American passport.

The snake he'd stolen was important enough that The Professor had switched continents to work with it.

And what about the Reptile Pub? Not only had Jacob worked there, but a place that creepy had to be doing something illegal. The Bartender had served a prison sentence for smuggling, yet he didn't have any recent arrests. Was he actually staying out of trouble, or had he convinced Jacob to do the dirty work?

"Holt?" Britt was squeezing my arm.

"Huh?"

"Do you have a headache?" Everyone at the table was watching me intently.

"No. I don't think so."

"It must be the mystery," Dad said extra loudly, his eyes darting over to Britt.

I suddenly regretted telling Dad about the missing ring. If he made too many strange comments, Britt would figure it out.

"Theft." I blurted the word before I fully comprehended its meaning.

"What's that?" Mom asked.

"This case isn't about murder; it's about theft." I began drumming my fingers against the table. "Think about it. Jacob stole a rare snake from the uni. Before the crime was officially reported, Jacob was killed. Someone else knew what he was up to."

"The snake's not the only thing he stole," Britt commented.

I raised an eyebrow. "My passport?"

Britt's lips tightened as she fought a smile.

"Are you suggesting I'd kill him for swapping our passports?"

Britt blinked her eyes innocently. "I would never think you were a murderer. But I wanted to make sure we had all the facts."

"Right," I said.

But she had a point. While I wouldn't kill Jacob for the passport swap, if I knew he'd taken my engagement ring, my motive for murder would be a lot stronger.

"A deadly snake worth killing for." Dad's eyes sparkled. He was finding this whole murder business a little *too* exciting.

Mom smiled at Dad. *"My kingdom for a snake."*

I rolled my eyes. My parents' flirting was always cringey, but why misquote Shakespeare?

Britt remained focused on the mystery. "Jacob didn't have ophidiophobia. He wouldn't have any problems with the reptile aspect of the theft."

She was right. Jacob clearly wasn't nervous around snakes. (But given that Jacob died from a snake bite, my fear of snakes was perfectly rational.)

"Would Jacob steal the snake by himself, or would he have a partner?" Dad asked.

He had a point. If Jacob was working with someone, they'd be the prime suspect. They might've arranged to meet him at a private location and killed him.

"You're both professors," Britt said. "How easy would it be to manipulate a student into committing a crime?"

Dad snorted. "I can't get them to do the required reading."

Mom's head tilted as she considered her answer. Finally, she settled on a somewhat vague "Depends on the student."

I wrapped my arm around Britt. "Jacob's girlfriend could be the accomplice."

Britt laughed. "It wouldn't matter how much I batted my eyelashes, I'd never convince you to steal a snake."

"I'd do anything for you," I practically growled—remembering a second too late that my parents were with us.

Mom either missed the romantic moment or skillfully ignored it. "Alexa cares about preservation. She wouldn't approve of endangered species leaving the country."

I nodded. "Not an accomplice. But she'd have motive, if she guessed what Jacob was planning."

"Then there's the bartender." Britt spoke matter-of-factly. Was she blushing? Or was I being paranoid?

Dad rested his chin in his hand. "The bartender has enough contacts in the snake world that I'm sure he'd be able to get a rough-scaled-midnight snake to the US without doing a passport swap."

He had a point. Yet there was something so pleasing about The Bartender being the killer—and I'm not just saying that because he was interested in Brittany.

"That means we're crossing the bartender off our list of potential accomplices?" Mom clarified.

"Unless..." I waited until everyone was leaning toward me. It was needlessly melodramatic, but I enjoyed myself. "What if The Bartender was Jacob's partner and Jacob decided to double-cross him?"

Three sets of eyes blinked at me.

"What if he had a plan for getting the snake out of the country, but Jacob decided to do his own thing?" I grinned. "It seems like Jacob wanted the snake for pharmaceutical research. Maybe The Bartender had other ideas."

"I love a good revenge killing," Dad said so matter-of-factly I couldn't tell if he was serious.

Mom frowned. "This little exercise hasn't exactly narrowed down our suspect list."

"That's right." I tapped my index finger on the table.

For possible motives, Alexa wanted to save endangered species. The Professor wanted to cure cancer. And The Bartender? Best I could tell, his only motive was money—but who doesn't love money?

"What if we asked them?" I suggested.

"Hm?" Britt asked mid-sip of water.

"You heard me," I said. "What if we summon the suspects to the Reptile Pub and figure out *whodunit*?"

"Does that mean you'd be guessing?" Mom sounded skeptical. "According to lawyers, you're never supposed to ask a question if you don't know the answer."

I winked. "Good thing we're not lawyers."

It was surprisingly simple to bring everyone together.

The Bartender should already be working at the pub. Mom texted Alexa and asked her to meet to go over lesson planning, while Dad called The Professor from the campus directory and invited him out for a drink. With The Professor being new to the area, he jumped at the chance to make a friend.

Dad wiped a bead of sweat from his forehead. "Professor Rhys was really excited. I shouldn't have lied to him."

Mom gave Dad's shoulder a squeeze. "I don't like lying to my student teachers, but a murder's a murder."

I wasn't quite sure what that meant, but with our plan in motion, there was no reason to ask.

Once we were all buckled up in the car and Dad was driving, I realized I should have chosen a better meeting location than the Reptile Pub. We'd already gone there today. What had possessed me to suggest going back? Surely we could've convinced The Bartender to meet with us at a less creepy location.

I glanced over at Brittany.

Dad was right. I should propose while we were in Australia. But was it better to propose without a ring or to go down on one knee with the *wrong* ring?

There were plenty of places in Melbourne where I could buy an expensive ring. But Britt deserved something special, not a desperation ring.

Even though I'd been loopy on Mom's natural sleep aids, how had I lost the ring? That was the most important thing I'd ever traveled with.

I must've groaned, because Britt rested her hand on my knee. "We'll figure this out."

For a panicked moment I thought she was referring to the ring. The next instant I felt like an idiot. Britt was talking about who killed Jacob.

Granted, I wanted to catch the killer, but with the missing engagement ring, I had bigger problems to worry about.

"What's the best strategy for getting our suspects to talk?" Dad asked.

"Alcohol," I muttered.

"We'll have to see how they respond when they're all in the same room together," Britt said.

Everyone together? That was horrible.

Why had I suggested this?

The last time The Professor and Alexa had been in a room together, their interaction hadn't been cordial. What would it be like adding a third person who knew Jacob, then multiplying that by adult beverages?

This was a bad idea.

What if bringing all the suspects together created a homicidal frenzy? Unmasking the killer by having them snap and kill more people would be problematic.

How would we explain that to the cops?

Sorry about the extra dead bodies, but we thought it'd be a good idea to round up the suspects and ply them with alcohol.

Definitely a mistake.

Unfortunately, I reached that conclusion right as Dad parked.

Ready or not, it was time to catch a killer.

Chapter 13

When we entered, The Professor sat on a stool facing the bar with The Bartender opposite him on the other side of the counter. There was no sign of Alexa.

The place was almost empty—aside from the countless snakes slithering around their cages.

The Bartender was leaning toward The Professor, and the two of them were quietly talking. Did they know each other?

"You're back," The Bartender said with a frown.

"Yeah," I said. "We shouldn't be long. You two know each other?"

The Bartender's jaw flexed. "Nah, yeah."

But The Professor didn't notice the undercurrent of tension. "Of course I know him." The Professor gave a happy sigh. "He runs my favorite bar. This is where I met Jacob."

Why hadn't I considered that The Professor would be a regular at the Reptile Pub? He'd gotten a doctorate studying snakes. Of course he'd enjoy this bar's terrifying ambience.

"Oh, Professor Jacobs." The Professor left his spot to shake hands with Dad. "I didn't realize this was a family affair."

That was the perfect time for Alexa to enter. Her eyes darted suspiciously around the room. "What's going on?"

I hesitated. It's not like I could outright say, *I'm pretty sure one of you murdered Jacob. All I need is the time to prove it.*

"Glad you could make it," Mom said, choosing to ignore Alexa's question.

"Why don't we all have a drink?" Dad suggested, taking a seat at the bar.

Britt wandered back to the cage with the suspected dead keelback. I followed, since I was a little lost. What was I supposed to do with the suspects now that they were all in one place?

"Do you see that?" Britt asked. "He hasn't moved at all."

She was right. The keelback was in the exact same place. Did the scales look drier?

I moved closer to the cage until my face was only an inch away from the glass. Suddenly a second snake's head popped up from a hole.

Surprised, I stumbled back, nearly knocking Britt over.

"Holt," she breathed. "Look at the pattern."

This snake didn't have the checkerboard skin of a keelback. Instead, its scales had blotchy markings. I leaned close to the cage, and sure enough, its pupils were a dark blue. We'd found the stolen rough-scaled-midnight snake.

I felt people watching us. Someone in the room had committed murder and hidden this snake at the bar. I didn't want them guessing our discovery.

Impulsively, I pulled Britt to me and kissed her as passionately as I could with an audience. Britt momentarily tensed before melting into the embrace.

My distraction worked so well, I forgot about everything but the woman in front of me. Britt finally broke away. Neither one of us spoke—we were too breathless.

Britt glanced purposefully at the cage behind me. I tilted my head for *No*. For now, that snake would be our little secret.

We joined the others at the bar. Dad handed us each a beer and then stared at me expectantly.

What was I supposed to do? Through a strange form of luck and logic, I've been able to solve a surprising number of crimes, but the process is much less methodical than a day at the office.

I was struggling. I'd like to blame the lack of planning on being upset over losing the engagement ring. But that wasn't the problem—the real issue was jet lag scrambling my brain.

With such a large audience, I decided to go after the low-hanging fruit.

"Did any of you know Jacob went to the airport to swap passports?"

I was met with silence. Like a bad enough silence that I checked behind me to see if a cobra was about to strike. No cobra.

"What Holt's trying to say..." Mom began before trailing off.

This wasn't fair. Rounding up all the suspects is a staple in old-timey murder mysteries. They made it seem simple. Why was it harder in real life?

If Juniper were here, she'd say something bold like, *I know one of you is the killer. You need to confess now.*

I'm not saying the killer would confess...but they might. Besides, Juniper could pull off saying that without making the whole room hate her.

I'd committed. It was too late to cancel. I needed to take a breath and plow through.

What if I did a breakdown of the crimes like those stuffy old detectives in Dad's dusty mysteries? Sure, I didn't know who the killer was, but I knew most of the setup. The solution must be staring me in the face. I'd get it.

"This baffling case first presented itself when the police arrived at the house to inform my dad I'd been murdered." I paused to let that sink in.

Britt was watching, her eyes sparkling. She didn't know where I was headed, but she'd be there for the ride.

"As we later found out, Jacob had swapped passports with me at the airport. He wanted an American passport to smuggle an endangered snake to the United States."

Alexa stood with her arms crossed, giving nothing away. The Bartender seemed more focused on the snake that was wrapping itself around his forearm. As for The Professor, he was leaning back against the bar, sipping his beer and taking it all in.

Based on the little I knew about body language, none of them was the killer.

"Jacob stole a rough-scaled-midnight snake from the university. When police discovered his body, he had a nonfatal head wound. Cause of death was venom from the stolen snake." I took a deep breath. *Here goes nothing.* "The killer took the snake with them."

That caught the suspects' attention. The Bartender winced, The Professor's face flushed, and Alexa stood even straighter.

"How could you know the killer has the snake?" The Professor cut in.

"You know where the snake is?" Mom asked.

The Professor's mouth fell open. "Well...I...uhh..."

Britt winked at me. I'd successfully gotten under the skin of one suspect. What would I do with the other two?

The Bartender crossed his arms.

I tried to ignore the snake slithering from his left wrist onto his other arm. "Snakes are sneaky creatures," The Bartender said. "It's hard to keep track of all of them."

Chills ran up my spine as I remembered the university jungle. How would anybody keep track of all the snakes inside?

As though reading my mind, The Professor said, "Each snake in my lab has a tracker. Once the police notified me, I checked the chip for the rough-scaled-midnight snake. The tracker stopped working near where Jacob was killed. A car must've run over it."

A strange hush fell over us. Was it stupid that we hadn't considered the university snakes were being actively monitored?

But even if Britt and I hadn't just discovered the missing snake, a car running it over was unlikely. Every suspect was aware of how valuable that snake was. They wouldn't let it slither into oncoming traffic.

Was The Professor covering for himself? Making up alternate stories about the snake being dead to keep people from finding the real snake?

The most obvious option for the tracker no longer working was that it'd been removed or disabled.

"Wait. That means you could have found Jacob and killed him." Alexa's voice cracked as she spoke.

"No!" The Professor's voice rose. "It couldn't have been me."

"Might as well confess now," I said. "It's obvious you were working with Jacob to smuggle the rough-scaled-midnight snake back to the States."

I may have been bluffing, but the terror in The Professor's eyes gave him away.

He set down his drink. "If you'll all excuse me, I'll be going."

The Professor began to leave, but The Bartender blocked his escape. "Jacob was a good kid. What did you get him involved in?"

The Professor gulped in a breath. The Bartender could be quite imposing when he wanted to be.

"I didn't make Jacob do anything," The Professor squeaked.

"Was it his idea to steal the snake?" The Bartender asked.

"Yes. No." The Professor's head fell. "Maybe? I don't know anymore."

All the air left the room at The Professor's confession.

"Excuse me." Dad moved toward the back of the bar. "The police will want to hear this."

Jacob and The Professor had been working together to get the snake to the US. But it didn't make sense. "Why move to Australia if you planned on sending the snake away?"

The Professor sighed wearily. "My impression of the research I could do with the rough-scaled-midnight snake differed from reality. One night at the bar, I started talking with Jacob. He kept pouring more drinks, kept asking questions. I told him about my wife, and he told me about his mom..." He shook his head.

"It's all right, mate." The Bartender gave his shoulder a quick pat.

The Professor shook his head. Life had weighed him down. "Jacob started telling me about a company in the US that was looking to fast-track a cure. A plan fell into place. When I sobered up, instead of changing my mind, I was positive I needed to go through with it. My wife is gone, but there's hope for Jacob's mom."

There was an uncomfortable amount of emotion in the room. I didn't know where to look.

"Why did you kill him?" Alexa's eyes were watery.

"I didn't." The Professor moved away, pointing a finger at all of us. "Don't think you can pin that murder on me."

"But you're the only person who could track Jacob using the stolen snake," I pointed out. It's not that I necessarily thought The Professor was the murderer, but he'd need to explain himself if he wanted to be off the hook.

The Professor rubbed a hand across his face. "The whole point of Jacob stealing the rough-scaled-midnight snake was to give me an alibi. The day he died, I was part of an all-day panel called Reptiles in the Modern World."

Ooph, that sounded dull. Could The Professor have committed murder after boring the entire audience to sleep?

"You have witnesses?" Mom asked.

"And it was filmed." The Professor's eyes were sad. "Now, if you'll excuse me, I'd like to get out of here before the cops arrive."

This time The Bartender let him pass. We all watched as The Professor walked out the door.

I couldn't help feeling bad for him. If Britt died, who knew what sort of tailspin I'd end up in.

"Holt," Britt prompted softly.

My attention shifted to Alexa and The Bartender.

And then there were two.

It wouldn't be a scientific approach, but could we catch the killer by flipping a coin?

Heads, Alexa was the killer. *Tails*, it's The Bartender?

"Shots on the house?" The Bartender offered. He set out a row of shot glasses and began pouring.

It was bizarre, but I couldn't help going along with it.

Present day, it's frowned upon to mix crime fighting with alcohol, but back in the days of detective noirs, a drink in hand was a necessity.

I coughed as tequila hit my throat and threatened to come out my nose.

We knew The Professor had helped Jacob with the snake theft, but he had an alibi for the murder.

What would The Bartender's or Alexa's motive be for killing Jacob?

"Are you going to cancel the police?" Alexa asked Dad. "The thief just got away."

"They'll still make an arrest," Dad said with a confidence I wished I shared.

I didn't even know if Jacob was murdered because of the snake theft. There could be an additional reason I'd yet to uncover.

There was one piece of evidence that did an excellent job of implicating The Bartender. It was time to reveal the ace up my sleeve.

I leaned across the bar and asked, "If you had nothing to do with the murder, how come you have the missing rough-scaled-midnight snake?"

I nailed the delivery. Total zinger.

"You know about that?" For once The Bartender's tough-guy persona cracked.

"Glad we didn't cancel the police," Mom commented.

"Call back and tell them we need animal control," Britt added.

The Bartender stood still. For once he didn't have a snake wrapped around him. "I swear to you, I didn't do this."

I didn't bother hiding my skepticism. "But you know the missing snake's in your bar."

"Of course I know." The Bartender's chest puffed up. "I can tell you the names and ages of every snake in here."

"You know there's a stolen, venomous snake that killed Jacob on your property, yet you had nothing to do with his death?" Britt's face was stern.

I *shouldn't* find that adorable. I *shouldn't* want to kiss her. Why was I this messed up?

That thought distracted me. I missed The Bartender's answer...My bad. It's likely all he'd said was an excuse about why he wasn't the killer.

"Holt, anything you'd like to add?" Dad asked.

"Sure, uh..." I cleared my throat. "When did you first notice the venomous snake was here?"

"After the cops stopped by," The Bartender admitted. "I couldn't shake the feeling that something was wrong. The pub wasn't right. When I inventoried the cages, I found my uninvited guest."

Dad let out a slow exhale—as a kid, that noise meant I'd majorly messed up.

When Dad spoke, he sounded calm. "You were aware a deadly, endangered snake was in your place of business, yet you didn't contact the authorities?"

The Bartender's jaw flexed, but he didn't answer.

"If you didn't steal the snake, weren't you afraid the killer was setting you up?" Britt asked. "They might've called an anonymous tip into the police."

The Bartender's face softened when he looked at Brittany. "I would've denied knowing about it." A vein in his temple began pulsing. "If I told the police, they'd try to pin Jacob's murder on me."

"Then what was your plan?" I asked. "You couldn't keep a deadly snake at your bar indefinitely."

The Bartender's jaw tensed, and he looked away.

"You were going to sell it!" Alexa accused.

The Bartender didn't answer...but that wasn't a denial.

"Do you remember anything suspicious happening on the day Jacob died?" Mom asked in an attempt to ease some of the tension.

The Bartender shrugged. "How would I know?" He tapped his hand on the bar, which summoned a small snake. "Actually, Alexa, didn't you stop by to see if Jacob was around?"

"No. That was the day before." Alexa tried to sound confident, yet her voice was higher than normal.

My eyes locked with Britt's.

Alexa's our killer.

But what was her motive, and how could we prove it?

The Bartender scratched his forehead. "No. It was the day Jacob died. I'm sure of it."

"Did she go near the cages?" I asked.

"Maybe..." He frowned. "It was a slow morning. After I told her Jacob wasn't here, she asked if I could check if he'd left a purple water bottle in his locker."

My focus was on Alexa as I asked, "That means there was a portion of time when Alexa was in this room by herself?"

"When you put it like that—yes." The Bartender leaned across the bar. "What could you want with a rough-scaled-midnight snake?"

Alexa's ears were pink. Before any of us could stop her, she bolted for the door. But a look out the window had her moving back inside. The cops must be in the parking lot.

In a few moments the cavalry would arrive. I could almost relax.

Problem was, they wouldn't be prepared to handle a reptile emergency, and Alexa knew it.

Since she couldn't walk out the front door, she moved back to the wall of snake cages.

I sucked in a breath as she opened the rough-scaled-midnight snake's cage and took him out. "Stay back," she warned.

This was turning volatile.

"Steady now," The Bartender called.

I couldn't look away from the venomous snake in Alexa's outstretched hands. Everyone in the room was one bite away from sudden death.

"Careful." I held my hands up—though it's not like Alexa could shoot venom from the snake like it was a gun.

"That's right," Britt's face had transformed into her paramedic mask. "No one wants to hurt this snake."

Alexa's wild eyes met Britt's. "You understand?"

"Yes," Britt answered.

I stared at Britt. What was she talking about?

Britt gave a comforting smile. "We all want what's best for that snake."

"You do?" Alexa's head darted around as she tried to look at everyone at once.

"Absolutely," Britt said. "Now, I think the snake is scared. How about all these extra people leave?"

My eyes widened. Britt was trying to get the hostages out of the bar—but if Britt thought I'd leave her alone with a woman wielding a venomous snake, she was wrong.

"Oh." Alexa's gaze rested on the door. "No. The cops are coming. I...I need someplace quiet to think."

Britt began, "How about—"

Alexa interrupted. "Come with me to the storage room."

Britt smiled. "That's a great idea."

When were the cops going to walk in? If they showed up, they'd put a stop to all of this.

Alexa began walking toward the storage room.

Should I try a running tackle?

No. Who knew where the snake would end up.

I cleared my throat. "Britt..."

Britt shook her head. She was about to willingly go into a storage room with a murderer wielding a deadly snake. It was a wonder my heart didn't explode. I loved Britt for being that brave—and hated that she wasn't more selfish.

It meant one thing.

I had to go too.

I couldn't leave Britt to face a killer by herself.

"Let me get the door," I offered and held it open for Britt and Alexa.

Britt was shaking her head even before she reached me. "You're not coming. There'll be a deadly snake inside."

I winked, trying to be playful, though my heart was hammering in my chest. "If you'll be there, I'll be there."

Britt tried to shove me back into the bar, but I'm stubborn and bigger than she is. Once I was in the storage room, I let the door shut. Now three humans and one venomous snake were trapped inside.

Was this a horrible idea? In a similar situation, I'd passed out. While in theory risking my life was romantic, the reality was that my presence could cause trouble for Britt.

My vision momentarily went hazy. What had I done? Would my love for Britt literally be the death of me?

Maybe it was the wrong time to bring it up, but I needed a distraction. "Is this because Jacob's a thief?"

Britt may have worked it out, but my brain was running slow.

Alexa shuddered.

"Having your partner choose to smuggle an endangered snake out of the country must've been upsetting," Britt said calmly.

Alexa's only reply was "We hadn't been dating that long."

This wasn't the time, given the murderer, the venomous snake, and the freezer full of dead mice, but Britt and I had been dating for an eternity. I needed to find a ring and get down on one knee as soon as humanly possible—assuming neither of us died in the next ten minutes.

"I thought Jacob was up to something," Alexa admitted. "I followed him. He was carrying this black bag. I wondered if it was a reptile bag, but I couldn't believe he'd smuggle snakes."

That black bag.

When this had all started, Mom had mentioned seeing Jacob with a tote bag. Then last night at the bar, Alexa had a black bag...She hadn't wanted to clean out Jacob's locker. She was hoping to retrieve the snake.

The rough-scaled-midnight snake made a hissing sound.

I jumped back, hitting the door. I *had* to start watching animal documentaries. That way I'd be more prepared for what animal body language meant.

Apparently, I hadn't overreacted. Britt asked, "Is there a cage?" right as the snake lifted its head and its body tensed. Alexa shrieked and threw the snake before it bit her.

In a panic from the deadly snake being freed, I clawed for the door. Britt and I were escaping.

Somehow, instead of the door, I pulled over a storage shelf. The shelf hit me on its way down and sent me sprawling. To make matters worse, the shelf not only blocked the door, but it also hit the light switch, casting the room in darkness.

I lay on the floor of a pitch-black room with a venomous snake slithering around.

Australia's the worst.

Chapter 14

Someone screamed—hopefully not me.

There was a rushing in my ears that quickly blocked out other sounds. It was hard to know, given the pitch-black room, but my vision was speckling, and I was in danger of blacking out.

The dim glow of a cell phone illuminated Britt's face before she tapped the flashlight, brightening the room.

"Can you move?" she asked.

I half nodded, making a gurgling sound.

"Let me help." It took Britt lifting the storage shelves for me to realize my legs were pinned.

I scrambled forward and got to my feet, spinning around wildly, trying to find the snake.

"Trust me," Britt said. "You'll be safe."

I didn't fully comprehend her words until I noticed she'd led me to the chest freezer and was opening the lid. "Get inside."

While I opened my mouth to refuse, no sound came out. Come to think of it, when was the last time I'd breathed?

"We'll fight about this later," she said.

My brain wasn't functioning properly. All I could do was shake my head.

"Snakes don't like cold," Britt explained. "Now get inside."

In a game of would you rather, the choice between sharing a freezer with hundreds of dead mice or risk getting fatally bitten by a snake, I'd tend to go the snake route. But Britt was there, telling me to throw my lot in with the dead mice.

I trusted her.

"I love you," I said, before climbing into the freezer and immediately dry heaving. It was *much* worse than I'd imagined.

There were plenty of sealed Styrofoam containers full of frozen carcasses, yet there were containers that had spilled open, and the whole space was filled with the creepy creatures.

If I survived, I was going to lock myself in my apartment and never see the light of day.

I held out my hand for Britt to join me in the freezer, but she'd turned away.

"Do you see it?" Britt asked Alexa.

"No." Alexa's voice wobbled. She sounded on the verge of tears. "Did I kill it? I couldn't live with myself if I killed it."

Odd. Alexa was upset over injuring a snake but seemingly didn't care about murdering her boyfriend.

Humans are weird.

"Personally, I'm more sad about Jacob." The words accidentally slipped out.

Alexa's chin jutted up. "It's people like Jacob who don't give endangered animals a chance to survive. Call it poetic justice, but it was right to get a little payback for generations of wrongs."

If the rough-scaled-midnight snake killed the three of us, would that also help the scales of justice?

"Uh-huh" was my noncommittal reply.

However misguided, Jacob had stolen the snake in an attempt to help his mom. He wasn't an ideal role model, but he also wasn't a cartoonishly evil villain.

"I couldn't believe it when I found Jacob with the rough-scaled-midnight snake." Alexa shook her head. "I told him not to work with that bartender. Dean Williams has no respect for living creatures and convinced Jacob it was better to sell animals than protect them."

I tried to meet Britt's eye, but she was too busy searching for the snake.

A new piece of the puzzle clicked into place. "That's why you hid the snake here. You blamed The Bartender and wanted him back in prison."

Alexa didn't answer. Her focus was on the ground as she tried to find the missing snake.

"But when the police searched the Reptile Pub, they couldn't spot the differences between the breeds." My words caused Alexa to stiffen—I must be on the right track. "You knew it'd look suspicious if you told the police to check again. That's why you stopped by to pack up Jacob's things. You were trying to get the snake back to the university."

Alexa gave a slight nod. "The world's a better place with Dean behind bars. I never considered the police couldn't spot a rough-scaled-midnight snake when it stared them in the face."

"You heard the professor." Britt's voice was soothing, and her attention remained on the floor. "This had nothing to do with Dean's smuggling. Jacob wasn't exploiting the snake for money. All he cared about was his mom."

"I didn't know." Alexa sniffled. She seemed to hesitate as doubt crept in, but the moment didn't last. "It's still wrong. He shouldn't have done it."

"That's right," Britt agreed. "Jacob was breaking the law."

While I'm sure we could have launched into a philosophical discussion about everyone's choices, a rustling cut short our conversation.

Britt's flashlight spun to the side as the search continued.

If you ever want to feel like an utterly useless human being, try standing safely in a freezer while your girlfriend and a murderer search a storage room for a deadly snake.

I should've helped, but my legs were shaking badly enough, I could barely keep myself upright, let alone climb out of the freezer.

Alexa held an empty cage, prepared to trap the snake once it appeared.

"Do you hear that?" Britt whispered. She turned around, and the lethal monster sat coiled near her feet. It hissed, and I swear venom sprayed across the room.

For a moment it was like the world around me froze. My life shrank to what was the most important—*Britt.*

Without consciously realizing what I was doing, I picked up a dead mouse and hurled it at the snake before it bit my girlfriend.

My aim was off. I didn't hit the snake, but I distracted it. The second mouse I threw hit along the side of the scales. I held a third mouse and was about to throw it when Alexa trapped the snake under the cage.

Everyone froze. Then Britt flung herself into my arms. "You touched dead mice to save my life."

I meant to say "Anything for you," but I doubt the words came out.

My vision went grainy as relief mixed with panic. I tried to pat Britt's back, but then felt the dead mouse that was still in my hand.

I gagged and dropped the mouse. I was in danger of puking all over the dead mice in the freezer—something no one would want to clean up.

I practically fell over the lip of the freezer and half crawled to the door. My hands were numb and tingly, and it was hard to get a good grip on the storage shelf that blocked the exit. But a new wave of nausea was surging through me.

I needed a bathroom. Now.

Britt or Alexa may have helped move the shelf. I don't know for sure. However it happened, fresh air and the bright light hit me.

The bar no longer held my parents or The Bartender, but was full of police.

There wasn't time to explain. I managed to say, "Bathroom," as I stumbled to the back of the bar.

At least no one tackled me—that'd be a move they'd immediately regret. I'd just shoved the bathroom's single occupancy door open when I heard "Was he bitten?"

They must be asking Britt.

There wasn't time to bother with the bathroom lock. My face was heating up, I was in a cold sweat, and my gag reflex was engaging.

I had to wash the dead mice off my hands. I sagged against the sink, getting as much soap as possible before scrubbing vigorously.

Hand soap would have to do. If there'd been bleach on the counter, I'd have poured that on—chemical burns were worth the price of cleanliness.

My hands were still sudsy when I dry heaved. That was my only warning. Immediately, I was kneeling by the toilet bowl, puking everything I'd eaten in Australia, every snack I'd had on the plane, that weird lunch in LA, and my last breakfast in Seattle.

I. Hate. Animals.

Reptiles, rodents, seahorses—anything that can kill me with a horrific disease.

I was sick for long enough, I couldn't be sick any longer. Sweat soaked my body, my leg was trembling from kneeling too long, and my hands were bracing myself against the toilet—not as bad as touching dead mice, but pretty disgusting.

"I thought puking was what you did on second dates."

I looked up from my spot on the floor to find Britt leaning against the doorframe. Her little scar by her eyebrow was defined, meaning she was worried. Yet she was smiling, pleased with herself for making a joke that went all the way back to our first date, when I thought she was a murderer.

There she was. We were alive. I was kneeling.

The woman I wanted to spend the rest of my life with was only a few feet away. It didn't matter that I'd lost the ring or looked disgusting. I had to ask if she'd be mine.

We'd almost died. I wasn't waiting any longer. I'd always planned on proposing today—granted, in a slightly classier setting, but today was the day.

Maybe it was crazy, and I'd probably regret it later, but I was on one knee...

"Marry me," I breathed.

"What?" Britt walked right to me, searching my face, worried she'd misheard.

"Brittany Asato, will you marry me?"

"Absolutely."

I would've jumped up to hold her in my arms, but Britt had tackled me to the floor—I really wish we weren't in a bar's bathroom.

I have no idea how long we'd been kissing when there came a knock on the doorframe.

We broke apart to find a police officer staring at us. "That's enough of that," she said in a no-nonsense way that made me feel like an eight-year-old. "You need to answer some questions."

After she left, I rolled up to a sitting position. My stomach gurgled, and I gasped.

Brittany instantly had one hand on my shoulder, the other brushing hair off my forehead. "What's wrong?"

I couldn't look at her. "We were kissing," I whispered, "after..." I tilted my head toward the toilet. "I haven't rinsed my mouth, let alone brushed my teeth."

Britt laughed, apparently too happy to be concerned with how disgusting I was.

She waited as I rinsed my mouth and washed my hands. Then my fiancée and I left the restroom to speak with the police.

CHAPTER 15

Back at my parents' house, I showered until the water turned cold.

I also used about half a tube of toothpaste to clean out my mouth.

The clothes I'd worn were thrown into the garbage.

I'd had on a favorite pair of shoes. It didn't matter. After the mice debacle, they were dead to me.

Britt waited for me at the kitchen table. She had a huge grin on her face. "There's my fiancé."

Once we'd suitably kissed, I wrapped my arm around her. "Sorry about the unconventional proposal. Believe it or not, I'd actually planned something more romantic."

Britt's laugh was playful. "I wouldn't have it any other way."

I shook my head. "The story you want to tell all your friends is *Holt proposed while he was kneeling at a toilet after puking his guts up*?"

"Absolutely. Every girl wants a unique proposal story." Britt snuggled closer. "Besides, the throwing up happened *after* you risked your life for me."

"You risked your life." I raised an eyebrow. "I was hiding in the freezer."

Britt began tracing the palm of my hand with her fingers. "That's not all you did."

For a moment I was happy enough that my heart might explode. Then I caught sight of Brittany's left hand, which was missing an engagement ring. "You know"—I touched her ring finger—"I was going to propose with my grandma's ruby engagement ring, but..." I cleared my throat. "It was lost somewhere between here and LA."

Britt's rib cage stiffened against me.

Was she trying not to cry?

But when I checked, her lips were quirked like she was trying not to smile.

Why would she laugh about a missing family heirloom?

Unless...she knew where it was?

Yikes.

"Brittany?" My voice was extra deep. "Do you have something to tell me?"

Britt's purse sat on the table. She reached over and dug inside before removing the velvet box that belonged to my grandma. "Looking for this?"

My mouth opened, but no sound came out. I took a deep breath and tried again. "How?"

Her eyes sparkled. "You gave it to me."

"When?" I ran a hand through my hair, trying to remember. "On the plane?"

Britt nodded. I had an annoying suspicion that if she tried to speak, she'd start laughing.

I racked my brain, trying to come up with why I'd handed the ring over. But Mom's *natural sleep aid* had erased my memory.

I opened the box and stared down at the ruby ring. "Did I...propose?"

Britt shook her head, and a giggle escaped.

"If I didn't propose, why would you have this?"

"You're not gonna like it," Brittany warned.

"I already don't like it."

"You were slumped against me, sound asleep, when suddenly you sat up. I thought you were going to be sick, but instead—" Brittany began laughing too hard to keep speaking. I sat there waiting for her to calm down enough to explain how I'd made a fool of myself.

"Instead..." Britt's words were swallowed by another round of laughter, this time hard enough that it barely made a sound.

I wanted to yell, *Get to the point already*. But yelling isn't a good way to begin an engagement.

Instead, I got Britt a glass of water. When I returned, she'd recovered enough to take a few sips. "Sorry," she said. "I might be jet-lagged."

"No argument here," I grumbled.

Brittany took a deep, steadying breath. "On the plane, you jolted up. Then you got this box out of your messenger bag and gave it to me."

I buried my face in my hands, afraid of what she'd say next.

"You told me very seriously that this was *Britt's engagement ring and I had to keep it a secret from her*."

I peeked through my fingers to stare at her. "I told you to keep the engagement ring a secret from yourself?"

Britt nodded. Her eyes sparkled, but she didn't laugh.

I groaned. "And after all that you still want to marry me?"

"One hundred percent."

I picked up the ring and slid it partway down my pinkie. I frowned. "You knew. This whole time, you knew where the ring was, and you never bothered to tell me."

"I thought you knew!" She shook her head. "We talked about it that first night."

What?

She saw my confusion. "I asked if you remembered our conversation on the plane."

Excuse me? The only thing Britt had asked about was...

"Kids. You asked if I wanted kids."

"Oh...the ring conversation happened later."

"Apparently."

Britt rested a calming hand on the back of my neck. "I tried a couple of times to get you to watch the video. I noticed you were off, but your mom kept saying it was jet lag."

I didn't want to fight, but I'd lost a year of my life worrying over her ring. "Why didn't you state plainly, *Holt, I have the engagement ring in my possession*?"

Brittany held up her hands like she'd been expecting this argument. "I told you on the plane that you might need a reminder when we landed. You refused. Insisted I couldn't tell a soul."

I leaned back in my chair. "If I wasn't in my right mind, why didn't you ignore what I said?"

"You made me promise."

"But—"

"And you filmed it, to *keep me honest.*"

I winced. Had I really said that? What a rude comment to make to the woman I wanted to spend the rest of my life with.

There'd been that video I'd taken on the plane, which I hadn't bothered watching...the video Britt had hinted I should watch. As much as I hated seeing it, I swiped through my phone and clicked on the video.

The camera jostled. It mostly faced Britt on the plane, but I was moving too much to keep her in focus.

"Promise?" a male voice in the recording said. It took a moment to recognize it was me.

Britt was glowing as she held the ring box. "I really think—"

"Nope!" The camera wobbled as I placed a clumsy finger on her lips. "You can't tell anyone until it's proposal time."

"All right, I promise."

The view tilted downward as I muttered about stopping the recording.

Britt said, "You'd better not get mad," in the background right as the video stopped.

I set the phone on the table. A strange silence filled the room.

Did I need to apologize?

She'd asked, then hinted at the conversation, kept getting me to look at my phone's camera roll. Ordinarily, I would've noticed what was happening, but my brain was too muddled.

I tugged at my hair. The engagement ring on my pinkie snagged on a stray curl.

What could I say to this incredible woman who'd agreed to spend her life with me? The ruby glinted up at me. It wouldn't be much, but it was time for a proper proposal.

I placed the ring back in the box and closed the lid before lowering myself to one knee. "Brittany Asato, would you do me the honor of being my wife?" I grinned as I opened the box.

Wait...Was this cringey or romantic? Whatever the case, I'd committed.

Britt pursed her lips, pretending to mull it over. "Believe me, I want to say yes—I really do—but I actually got engaged earlier today."

A warmth spread across my chest. I was so happy, it was hard to pretend to be disappointed.

I smacked a hand to my forehead. "You're sure you want to stick with that guy? He didn't propose with a ring."

Brittany lightly traced her finger along the ring. "How about I stay engaged to the first guy, but I keep this ring?"

"Sounds perfect." My voice was more of a rumble. Carefully, I removed the ring from the box and slid it onto Britt's ring finger. My attempt to get her finger size had succeeded.

The ring fit perfectly.

I kissed her finger, then her hand. Then realized I was wasting time and went straight for her mouth.

"I love you," I murmured a while later.

"Right back at you." Britt gave me a playful shove, and I sat in the chair beside her.

Probably for the best that we took a break from kissing. I never knew when Mom might barge into the room.

I wrapped my fingers through hers and tilted her hand to get a good view of her engagement ring.

"It's perfect." Britt's gaze was on the ring.

My chest expanded. I'd known this was the ring for her.

Britt was everything. She needed a ring full of history and love, not some flashy trinket from a diamond shop.

This moment felt right. The two of us together.

"Any chance when we tell the proposal story, we only mention the proposal in the kitchen? Juniper already thinks I'm not romantic. She might drop dead if she heard I proposed in a public restroom without the ring—or a breath mint."

That last bit was a joke, but Britt was chewing her lip, and the scar by her eyebrow was creased.

"You okay?"

"Um..." Britt tucked an invisible strand of hair behind her ear. "Any chance we keep this a secret?"

Keep what a secret? How I proposed seconds after puking my guts out? The fact I'd lost the ring? Or that I'd hidden in a freezer while my future wife went snake hunting?

When I didn't answer, Britt began talking in a rush of words. "I know a *secret engagement* sounds scandalous, but it'll only be for a few weeks—until Paul and Sienna get married. They've gone through so much. I don't want to steal any attention from them."

I leaned back in my chair and crossed my arms. "But it's not a secret. Everyone in my family—and Darren—knew I was proposing. What am I supposed to say? *Ask me after Paul's wedding.*"

"It's fine if your family and Darren know. But can we wait on telling anyone else until after the wedding?"

I didn't like it.

But since apparently I'd told Britt on the airplane about my plans to propose, she'd had days to think about it.

While I didn't want to overshadow Paul and Sienna's big day, I couldn't shake the feeling that Britt wasn't telling me the whole truth.

"Is that the only reason?"

I hadn't meant to sound accusatory, but before I could apologize, Britt's brown eyes were peering straight into mine. "You're right," she said. "Their wedding isn't the whole truth." She broke the eye contact, suddenly happy to stare at anything that wasn't me. "Mom didn't get a good first impression of you. If we show up as an engaged couple, she won't get the chance to see how great we are together."

A weight settled around my chest. "You think your mom seeing us together as a regular couple will make her like me?"

Britt shrugged. "I hope so."

"Fine," I agreed. "I'll do it."

I could do it. I could be part of a secret engagement.

What could go wrong?

Will an unexpected corpse be Holt's biggest problem, or will it be his future mother-in-law? Read *A Not So Shallow Grave* to find out!

Ready for a Holt Jacobs snack-sized mystery? Sign up for my newsletter at *lilystirling.com* and receive a copy of *Holt Jacobs & The Mystery Of The Missing Sunglasses,* plus delightful every-other-week emails.

AWESOME!

Congrats, my friend! You've just completed Holt's international mystery. :)

It would really help me (and future readers) if you took the time to rate and review this book. This helps let potential readers know if this is the perfect story for them.

Now, to important business. (I promised my mom I'd do this.)

While pseudo-researching on YouTube, I stumbled upon nonvenomous keelbacks and venomous rough-scaled snakes. They're real, look similar, and are native to Australia.

...Slight problem. According to the internet, while rough-scaled snakes are venomous, their species is only attributed one fatality.

I wanted my snake to be more lethal.

Initially, I planned to use the keelback snakes and make up a different highly venomous breed (while shamelessly using all the descriptors of rough-scaled snakes). Mom informed me that wouldn't do.

I'll save you all the back-and-forth discussions we had on this topic, but the end result is that I made up the *extra venomous* rough-scaled-midnight subspecies.

Otherwise, I did my best to give accurate snake information...though I'm by no means a *reptile-ologist* and my research consisted of random internet searches.

If you'd like to hear more about me and my writing process—plus read Holt's airport mystery, *Holt Jacobs & the Mystery of the Missing Sunglasses*—be sure to sign up for my newsletter at *lilystirling.com*.

[Cue thematic background music]

Next up, Holt's returning to Amelia's Haven in *A Not So Shallow Grave*. Holt not only has to hide his engagement, but a routine body retrieval unearths a second corpse, and brings the return of an old enemy. I'm so excited about this one!

Happy reading!

~ Lily Stirling

Acknowledgements

Thank you to my wonderful production team!

Developmental Editor ~ Kristen Weber
Copyeditor ~ Penina Lopez
Cover Designer ~ Mariah Sinclair

A huge thanks goes to my family for all your love and support. I'm blessed to have you in my life.

Massive shoutout to Anita B. and Julie Z. for answering questions about Australia. I so appreciate the time each of you took to answer my strange questions about your continent.

Also, thanks to T-Ray for recommending the TV show My Life Is Murder. Since season one took place in Melbourne, watching it counted as *research.* (Sadly, the show moved to New Zealand after season one, so I lost my *research* excuse and continued watching for pure enjoyment.)

Thanks to Alessandra, Terezia, Eva, and my author friends at Inkers Mastermind. It's been incredible to be part of such a supportive writing community.

Finally, thank *you* for reading my book and all the back matter. I hope you love Holt and Britt's engagement story as much as I do!

Until next time!

Lily Stirling

About the Author

Lily Stirling is the author of the Holt Jacobs Mystery series and a co-author for the Moonshine Girls Mystery series.

She has spent a quarter of a century living in the Pacific Northwest. Lily was born in Idaho, but her family moved to Washington around the time she could read chapter books.

Mysteries have always delighted her, from listening to The Hardy Boys on car trips to watching episodes of Psych.

As for sarcastic families, when she's not writing about one, she's living in one.

Holt Jacobs Mystery Series

A Not So Shocking Murder

A Not So Rustic Retreat

A Not So Rosy Vintage

A Not So Cozy Christmas

A Not So Simple Seminar

A Not So Happy Camper

A Not So Perfect Proposal

A Not So Shallow Grave

Holt Jacobs isn't for everyone. He's a sarcastic introvert who can never get quite enough coffee. Becoming a sarcastic sleuth was unexpected, but as an engineer, Holt is used to solving puzzles.

Moonshine Girls Mystery Series

Murder & Moonshine

Poison & Pumpkin Spice

Heartbreak & Hooch

Freedom & Firewater

Moonshine Girls Davie Carter, Fenn Everhart, and Daisy Mae Harper met over moonshine and have been friends ever since. They'd planned on distilling, transporting, and selling illegal hooch but keep stumbling over crimes and solving mysteries.

The Moonshine Girls Mystery Series are intertwined anthologies written by Lily Stirling, Bellamina Court, and Jess Corbeau.

www.ingramcontent.com/pod-product-compliance
Lightning Source LLC
LaVergne TN
LVHW050958080826
845145LV00009B/2344

* 9 7 8 1 9 6 7 4 0 2 0 2 1 *